THE LEGENDS OF DOTHVERA

REBECCA MILLS

Printed in the United Kingdom

First Printing, 2020

Illustrated by Richard Newnham
Front Cover design by Ceri Newnham

ISBN 978-1-8380106-7-6

Published by Artbully Ltd, UK

To Joshua, Oliver, Zak and Amelia
"May life continue to guide you along the
path of greatest adventure."

To
Victoria,

I hope you enjoy
reading this as much
as I enjoyed writing
it.   Best wishes

iii

PROLOGUE

"Now little Bobby, I think it's about time you started to take responsibility for your room, hmm?" Responsibility was a big word for young Bobby.

"I think it's about time you started tidying your room,"

The boy looked up at his mother, all wide-eyed and innocent looking. He had recently turned ten and he didn't quite understand why his mum wanted everything so tidy and clean in his bedroom. After all, Bobby didn't know that underneath all that dust, creatures of all kinds lurked and hid. Under all those piled up clothes, spiders would build their nests to wait on unsuspecting creatures and devour them. Bobby was only ten after all. How could he know all that?

As he tried to listen to his mum, his mind wandered and he slipped into a daydream. While his mum spoke about the importance of a clean and clear room, Bobby was in a mystical world full of monsters and he was battling a boglet in his mind. A boglet, as Bobby and his friend Zak had mentioned to his sister one day, was a creature that lived in bogs, very similar to a goblin and not unlike an ogre in size. Of course, Bob's mum wouldn't understand how important it was to learn the art of battling boglets.

"So, from today, I'd like you to begin cleaning your room, do you remember where we keep the polish Bobby?" Bobby nodded, but he hadn't heard his mother telling him where the polish was kept. He wasn't sure he even knew what polish was.

"Okay fab, you're growing up now Bobby, it's time to start learning how to look after things, tell you what, you go up to your room, I'll get the polish and show you what to do. Okay?"

Bobby nodded. He was good at that. Nodding in the right places and looking like he understood. He didn't always understand but, hey, at least only he knew that.

The young boy peered around his room. A library of books was piled high on a shelf and in the corner sat his computer, surrounded by toys of all kinds. In the middle of the floor was a mat that was hidden under clothes and toys and pictures of boglets that Bobby and his friend Zak had drawn. 'Ugly creatures they were,' thought Bobby as he picked up the picture.

Forgetting what his mum had said, he grabbed another piece of paper and began writing the word boglet "b-o-g-l-e-t" he said and smiled and sat on top of his clothes hill and started daydreaming again.

"Bobby!" yelled his mum when she walked into the room to find her son sitting on top of the messy floor, playing grab a boglet with his toys again. Bobby jumped up.

His mother handed him the polish. "Bobby, until this room is cleaned up, you will not be going out to play! Is that clear?" Bobby nodded. His mother didn't understand at all, but he knew when she spoke in that voice that it was game over. It was time to take on some re-spon-sib-ility.

The young boy looked at his room and didn't know where to begin. He looked up at his ornaments on the windowsill. "I can polish those" thought Bobby and walked over.

There was a photo frame of a picture of Bobby and his dad out at dinosaur world, a few books and an ornamental dragon that was covered in a thick layer of dust.

Bobby had remembered his grandfather giving him that dragon. It was a dark red dragon, covered in scales and its wings were so thick with dust that they were hardly visible, the dragon was sitting on ornamental books and was stood as though it was guarding them.

Bobby picked up the dragon, held it in his hand and almost fell into a daydream again, about dragons this time, flying through the sky, swooping and soaring. But understanding the seriousness of his mother's wishes, the young boy stopped himself mid-daydream and decided to do what was right.

He proceeded to dust the dragons wing gently trying to get into the gaps and clear off the dust and just as soon as he had begun, the room began to spin. Bobby felt his head spinning round and round, it felt like he was on the fastest merry-go-round ever. He closed his eyes as he felt himself rush further and further around, and getting dizzier and dizzier, it was as if his feet were lifting off the ground. All of a sudden, he came to a stop and landed on his bottom on the floor. 'How strange' thought Bobby, still with his hands covering his eyes.

Thinking he must have lost his balance somehow and landed on the floor in his room, Bobby opened his eyes, expecting to see his bedroom just as he'd left it.

But he was somewhere else. The floor beneath him was white with grey speckles. It was almost as if a light grey sand had been dusted over it. As Bobby tried to get used to his surroundings, he heard a huge thunderous crack that pounded down upon him from above. In amazement and curiosity, he looked up to see the large incredible beast before him.

With a thunderous roar the dragon shook its huge wings expelling the dust from all of its crevices. Bob opened his mouth wide in shock.

"Who-o a-are you?" the boy asked, stuttering his words.

"What was that?" the dragon roared, and then began to cough and splutter fire and dust into the air. Bobby covered his head with his arms as charred dust sprayed over him.

"Wait a minute, who summoned me?" said the dragon with a croaky voice, "Was that you down there?" the dragons long neck stretched downwards, Bobby lifted his arms to find the dragons face very close to his own.

Then he noticed something. This dragon looked exactly like the one he was just dusting only a moment ago, but it couldn't be. Could it?

"Speak up my son, I don't have all day!" exclaimed the dragon boldly. Bobby could feel the heat from its breath it was so close.

"I-I s-said..."

"Yeeeeees" encouraged the dragon

"W-who who a-are you?" Bobby gulped nervously.

"Aaaah, nice to meet you. I am Dothvera, guardian of the books of Shamlu,"

Dothvera tapped the incredibly huge books below him that he was perched upon. They were leather bound, and locked at the edges. Nothing like any book that Bobby had ever seen.

"Guardian of books?" Bobby's' mind asked. What could that be? And why? And, where was he? And why did this dragon look so much like the one on his windowsill. There were too many questions. He couldn't possibly ask them all at once. Before he had a chance to even ask one of these questions, Dothvera spoke again.

"And who, might I add, are you?"
Bobby looked up.

"I am Bobby, Bobby Bobcat,"

"Bobby Bobcat, but you look so..." the dragon looked confused.

"...young" he said.
'Young?' thought Bobby.
"Well, I'm actually considered quite tall for my age," he answered.

"Wait a moment, you are Bobby Junior! The Bobby Junior!"
"What?" asked Bobby.
"Never mind, how did YOU get here?" asked the dragon.

"I don't know, I was polishing my room and I-I'm not sure,"

"Well, I suppose we'll just have to find a way back,"
Find a way back? What was this dragon talking about? Bobby looked around once again to determine what exactly had happened. He kicked the sand beneath his feet to find a bright white floor. He walked around a little and then he spotted it. His bedroom was right in front of him, but he was...

"I'm on my windowsill, but... but... I... how?"

Bobby walked towards the image in front of him until he came to a frightening stop. He was stood at the edge of his windowsill looking out over the vast space in front of him. He was tiny and the room was... huge. What had happened?

CHAPTER 1

"Boglets are real??"

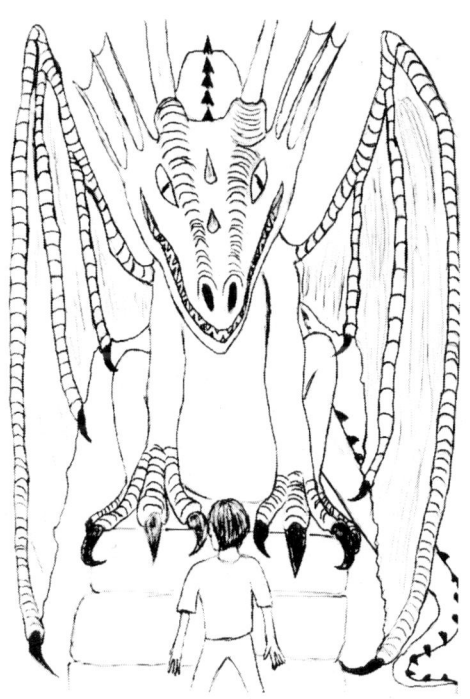

Bobby could not believe it. What would his mum think? She would soon notice he wasn't there and begin to worry. What could he do?

"Are you alright Bobby Junior, you seem so..." the dragon stretched his neck out even further placing his head next to Bobby's as they looked out over the huge bedroom that reached far into the distance.

"I'm so confused." Bobby answered. One minute I was there and now... What if I never see my family again?"

"Oh, there is a way back," answered Dothvera, hoping to make his newly found friend feel better.

"I think it might be in these books, but I don't have the key and we're not in a safe place, here in the 'in between' if I move the Boglets will surely..."

"Stop, did you just say the Bog...?"
"Boglets, yes, awful creatures, for a moment I thought you may have been one,"
"Me?"

"Indeed, after all they are very similar to humans in size and shape, but rather different when you get up close, don't you think?"

Bobby opened his mouth in shock. His mum had always told him that Boglets didn't exist, he was beginning to wonder whether the stories his grandfather had always told him were simply fairy-tales, and there was no truth in them at all. But here he was with a dragon right in front of him, in plain sight, and talking about Boglets. Bobby had to ask questions now.

"I thought they were like goblins, very ugly and naughty,"

"Naughty?" said Dothvera, "they are the most feared creatures in this world. That is why I am here to protect our secrets, the secrets of Shamlu" said Dothvera tapping the books once again.

"Shamlu" Bobby repeated.

"Yes, that's where you are Bobby, Shamlu. Well, nearly." the dragon winked at the boy, as if he were letting him in on a secret that only the two of them knew.

Bobby's mind was running wild. This all seemed so odd, so strange. Something that weirdly made Bobby feel safe however was this massive fire breathing creature in front of him. Dragons were often said to be dangerous due to their sheer size and strength but as Bobby's grandfather had told him time and time again, they were often very mistaken creatures because they were just like us.

Some were bad and some were good. Dothvera seemed like a very nice Dragon. He spoke a little like Bobby's grandfather and reminded him of him. That made Bobby feel very safe indeed.

"So, um, can you move from there?" asked Bobby looking at the heavy books beneath the dragon.

"Absolutely not!" said Dothvera, extremely offended at the thought, "Why, that would be preposterous, disgraceful! Absolutely disgraceful! How could you even utter the idea of it!" the dragon moved away from Bobby and sat up with his wings held together tightly. "NO." he said with a stern look in his eye.

"Maybe you are a Boglet after all," said the dragon, intending to offend the boy. After all, the 'in between' was quite different from his home. Dothveran dragons rarely visited this strange place, and they never normally entered this part of their world alone. Who knew what magical powers Boglets had here?

Bobby turned around and got up. He wasn't a Boglet, he had never even seen one. He didn't understand this world. The books were locked and looked mighty heavy. He couldn't imagine something as small as a Boglet, if that's how small they were, could even get through those books. He couldn't even imagine getting to the top of them safely.

Bobby sat down wondering what to do next. He wanted to explore this world a little more but Dothvera was the only person, well, Dragon that he knew here. He decided to stay a while and ask a little more first.

"Dothvera!" he called up to the dragon who was still sitting sternly in place.

Dothvera ignored him.

"How do I get home?" he called, "Please!" cried the boy desperately. Dothvera felt for the child. He remembered when he first met Bobby's grandfather how much he didn't understand and how kind Bobby Bobcat was spending hours with him explaining about the world of giants. He was treated well by the original Bobby and now if this really was Bobby Bobcat's grandson, he owed it to the boy to help him. He owed it to Bobby Senior to care for him.

Bobby decided that if he couldn't get an answer, he would set out to find it himself and so he proceeded to walk away from the dragon.

"Wait!" called Dothvera. The young boy walked faster.

"Wait! No! You can't go out there on your own!"
Bobby was nearing the edge of the windowsill,
which was next to some shelves in his room. As
he prepared to jump, he was stopped still when he
heard a loud crack and Dothvera landed in front
of him.

"NO!" the dragon roared. Bringing his wings
down in front of Bobby.

"Wait, you said you couldn't move!" shouted
Bobby, upset that the dragon had lied to him.

"I'm not supposed to!" called out Dothvera.
Dothvera looked Bobby sternly in the eyes.
Bobby stared back.

"I need to find out what's going on and where I
am and how I get back to my world, don't you
understand that?" Bobby yelled up to the dragon

above him with a sadness in his eyes. He was already missing the sound of his mother's voice and her presence in the house, downstairs pottering around doing, whatever mothers do.

He liked that, it made him feel safe. Now he felt lost. Everything was so new and that scared him. Dothvera sighed a warm sigh and noticing the sorrow in the young boys' eyes, decided to advise him, as his grandfather had often advised the dragon.

"Look Bobby, I understand that you're afraid, but remember fear is never a good thing to listen to. You are better off here safe with me than you are running off into a world you have no idea about. I always remember your grandfather had that spirit for adventure, but he knew this world Bobby. He spoke our language and learned the secrets of Shamlu before he headed off out there and explored it. I promise that I will take you out there but first I must inform the other Dothvera that you are here, yes? Will you let me do that and let us figure this out. Firstly, I don't know how you got here, and secondly; I don't know if you are permitted to access the books. If you are, we will look through them and see what can be done, okay?"

Bobby nodded. Together they walked back to the books and Dothvera stood upon them once again.

"So, Dothvera?"

"Yes, my lad,"

"What are the other Dothvera you mentioned, who are they?"

"Why, they are my brothers, I am Dothvera Ferrucio (fire) and I have three brothers. Dothvera Velara (water), Dothvera Cherama (earth) and Dothvera Potentioh (air). We are the Dothvera ov Dragero, the Doorway Dragons or, of course, Dragons of Doorways," Dothvera looked proudly at Bobby. He knew that the Dothveran Dragons were the most important dragons of all, as they were protectors of the doorways of Shamlu.

"So, you are doorway dragons? What does that mean?"

"Well, it means that I am especially important to Shamlu. I protect it. I am a protector Bobby, I protect the doorways to our world, the doorway you have just entered through."

"Doorway?" replied Bobby, looking around him.

"Yes, you have just entered through a doorway that leads to the place that lies in between your world and ours. Many do not enter this way, it is rarely opened, the last person to get in this way was…" the dragon stopped speaking and stood still staring at Bobby, "well it doesn't matter," the dragon said as if he realised that he had been saying too much already to the boy. After all, in this part of his world, a dragon couldn't be too careful.

"So, how did you meet my grandfather?" asked Bobby, completely unaware of what Dothvera had just almost said. The dragon was pleased at the distraction.

"Ahhh, Sir Robert J Bobcat, a fine man, a very fine man indeed, I met him as I met all keepers of Dothvera, when his predecessor moved to vethreaah,"

"To what?" asked Bobby.

"To the land of another life, vethreaah, I think it is pronounced dearth to your kind,"

"Dearth?" Bobby stopped for a second. "You don't mean, death?" Bobby said.

"Yes, that's it, sorry Bobby it has been a while, your grandfather hasn't been here for quite a long time,"

"How long?" asked Bobby.
"Oooh, about 235 years I think,"

"TWO HUNDRED AND THIRTY-FIVE YEARS?" exclaimed Bobby loudly. His grandfather had only been alive for eighty-six years, how could that have been possible?

"But he was only eighty-six years old Dothvera, how could he have been away for two hundred and thirty-five years?"

"Oh, I guess time works differently around here Bobby, aah yes, he did mention it a long time ago, he said that whenever he went away with me on journeys his family wouldn't miss him at all. He would feel homesick but it was like he'd never even gone when he came back, or as if he'd only been away for a few minutes, and he was sometimes on journeys with me for what must have been weeks,"

"Weeks?" the boy said, still shocked at everything he had just heard.

"Weeks, it is weeks isn't it? I believe that's what Sir Bobcat said to me. You see we don't have weeks ourselves. We have years and months and days and that is it. Some years are longer than others, some months are shorter than others and some days last for a lot longer than one cycle of Shamlu,"

"So, do you have nights at all?"

"Nights?" Dothvera asked, almost as if he had never heard the word before.

"Yes, they are dark and the stars, I mean..." said Bobby stopping to think, "the bright lights come into the sky, that thing above us,"

"Oh, Bobby, I know what a sky is for goodness sake! But I think you are talking about the nostera, that doesn't come around often my son, it is a rare thing, but I have seen a few nostera in my lifetime,"

Bobby had to take some time to sit down and take all this in. What Dothvera had said was right. He didn't know anything about this world he was in. Shamlu seemed like such a different place to home. He began to wonder what kind of adventures his grandfather had been on with Dothvera and how many of the stories he had told young Bobby were true. Did he ever meet pirates or pigs that spoke, and did he ever battle with a giant tyrannosaurus rex? Bobby always believed these stories were simply tales his grandfather had told him, but were they? They always did sound believable. Perhaps that's because Bobby Senior or Sir Robert J Bobcat had been doing these things in Shamlu on his journeys with Dothvera. It was all too much to take in.

CHAPTER 2

Elvathrah

"Bobby, I need you to tell me how you think you got here?" asked Dothvera. Bobby thought for a moment, all he knew was that he was in his room one minute and he was this tiny human in front of a dragon the next. What help was that?

"How did this happen?" Dothvera asked again, gesturing into the air with his huge claws that seemed too big for one small boy to have even imagined before seeing them up close. Bobby thought about his answer.

"I don't know. One minute I was there, now I am here, and I didn't do anything to make it happen, it just… it just did,"

"Ok," Dothvera said confused about what he was supposed to say to his brothers about this unique young boy. Hopefully, they could help him in some way.

"Maybe if you tell me what you were doing the exact moment that 'it' happened,"

Bobby paused to think about what was happening the moment he picked up the dragon.

"Well, I was asked by mum to clean my room and then I came into the room and picked you up and polished some of the dust from your, elbow, I mean um wing, and then..."

"Wait, did you say my el-bo-oow? What's a 'elbow' Bobby?"

"*An* elbow," Bobby corrected the dragon. "Well it's connected to the arm it's kind of..."

"Oh? connected to the arm, where?"
"Here." Bobby said poking out his elbow.

"Elvathraaaah!" the dragon said, suddenly showing complete understanding of the situation.

"Hmm?"

"That's called my Elvathrah Bobby. It's where the wing breaks into two, much like your arm here," The dragon lifted Bobby's elbow into the air with the tip of his wing.

"Elvathrah." Bobby said.

"Now, I understand what has happened," nodded the dragon "...but usually the only person who has ever entered Shamlu like that is Sir Robert J Bobcat, your grandfather. He was the only person who knew about my Elvathrah and he was meant to be the only person who held the magic inside him to open the doorway without a key."

"So, what does Elvathrah mean in my language?" asked Bobby.

"Dragon's Elbow I suppose," the dragon answered, as if it were obvious.

"Is there a book that teaches the language of Shamlu Dothvera?" Bobby asked, wanting to learn more about the words he was hearing. In school, he had learnt a little of a language called Welsh but only a few words. This language was much more complex.

"I believe that your grandfather used to make notes of what each word meant, we taught each other a lot of words. He was the first person to really ask those kinds of questions. Not many of the keepers of Dothvera visited here, they mainly kept us safe and hidden, but your grandfather, he was a fine man, a fine man indeed and he was the first to be knighted by the Dothvera. He loved this world as much as his own, and he explored it more than anyone before him, Bobby."

Bobby couldn't believe how much time his grandfather had spent exploring this world and it seems like he had been the first to truly do it. Did he know this? Did he realise what a hero he was believed to be in the eyes of this dragon? Bobby wished he could go back to his world and tell his grandfather, but he couldn't any longer. He did miss his grandfather so much, but since meeting Dothvera it was almost like he was finding out more about him than ever before. He wondered if Bobby Senior had known this. He wondered if he had left the Dothvera with young Bobby for a reason. Did he know this was going to happen?

Suddenly Bobby remembered that his grandfather had also left him a journal for him to write in. It was somewhere in his room, but it had nothing written in it. Bobby remembered looking in the journal and finding a message from his grandfather in the front, something like, "This is yours now Bobby, keep it safe". Bobby did wish his grandfather were with him to help him today. As the boy's mind grew active, thinking about the days with his grandfather, Dothvera Ferrucio went absolutely silent. Everything went completely still for a moment and then the dragon stood upright.

"My brothers request a conversation with you, Bobby." Bobby looked shocked at this news.

"But how do they know about me?"

"I sent them a letter." Bobby knew the dragon hadn't written a letter. He would have seen it happening, the largest creature he had ever seen was right in front of him.

"But how? And when?"

"You do ask a lot of questions young Bobby," the dragon answered, "but we don't have time for explanations right now. C'mon jump on!" the dragon said, placing his large head on the floor in front of the boy.

"What?"

"We're off to meet my brothers Bobby." Bobby couldn't believe his eyes. Was he about to ride a dragon?

"Well c'mon, or it'll be nostera before we get there!" Bobby jumped up onto the dragon's head and sat in between his ears, it wasn't what he was expecting. The dragons head was hard and strong, just like the ornament he had been polishing that day. This was a real live, enormous, ornamental dragon!

Dothvera grabbed hold of something in the air and all of a sudden it turned into the biggest set of chains you could ever imagine. They appeared as if by magic, Bobby could see that they were attached around the set of books Dothvera had been perched on all this time.

"Hold on!" Dothvera called and Bobby grasped onto the dragon's head as tightly as possible as the pair of them lifted into the air above his bedroom and began their journey dragging the books behind them. Bobby lifted his head into the air to see what was happening around him, he was just about hanging on, but he had to see this.

Dothvera swept down across his room and past his computer, over the shelves and up into the air. He then soared towards the bedroom door and Bobby thought he was going to hit it, he was so close, but he swept upwards eventually spinning Bobby until he was upside down on top of the dragon. The boy closed his eyes and felt his stomach turn as Dothvera laughed happily, with the excitement of it all. Dothvera was building up his speed. Bobby only realised this when he noticed the small top window in his bedroom that was always left open and Dothvera was heading towards it. He spun around once more and just as he did, he lifted the books up to his feet put his wings out straight and flew out of Bobby's bedroom window.

"Woooooooohoooooo!!" cried out Dothvera sweeping and diving through the air. He was loving this. Since he had been on adventures with Sir Robert, he had built up a desire to fly and to explore. All these years he had been waiting for this day, for the doorways to be opened again, for his world to become true again. He had waited for someone with a strong heart to step through into Shamlu and teach him even more.

He had forgotten what it felt like to be this alive, and to be this free in the 'in between'. It had been a long time since he had explored this incredible world of giants. This was bliss!

Bobby held on and watched as the world he knew drifted past below him. Although he was smaller and the mountains were bigger, as he swept upwards and downwards, everything looked so small. The mountains, the oceans, the valleys and trees.

Bobby had never even been on a plane. He had never travelled this far before. He hadn't realised what was outside his window, what existed beyond his school playground. This world of his was... beautiful. Suddenly what seemed like the most frightening thing he could have done, felt calm and peaceful. Bobby was there taking it all in, enjoying the rush of the breeze, looking out over the clouds, and then he noticed a bird that swept in alongside him and Dothvera. Up against them both, the bird looked larger than any other bird in the world.

Bobby wondered if it would try to swat them or eat them both, but it was almost as if this beautiful bird could not even see them. Or if it could, it was totally oblivious.

"A hawk I believe young Bobby!" called out Dothvera, he remembered when Sir Robert had told him all about the flying creatures of his world.

"Why can't he see us?" shouted Bobby.

"No need to shout my boy," called out Dothvera, "you're right by my erotha,"

"Erotha?"
"Oh, um, my ear Bobby, please don't shout. I can hear you perfectly, and the reason why the bird cannot see you or hear you is because he is in your world and not ours. Right now, we are right in the middle of worlds,"

"Really?" asked Bobby. He didn't quite get it. How could someone or something not see what was right in front of it? That was certainly very strange.

The journey felt much shorter than it appeared. Maybe it was the sheer speed of a dragons flight, or maybe it was just that Bobby was so enthralled by what was happening that he didn't feel time pass at all, but it felt like no sooner than they had left Bobby's bedroom, they began to soar above a street with old style houses that were very close together.

"Here we are." said Dothvera, as they flew up to a shop that had written in old style lettering 'Ye Olde Ornamental Store', on a sign that hung from the wall.

Bobby, who had almost fallen asleep during the latter part of the journey was startled by a loud crack against the floor as Dothvera landed inside the store. He jumped up to find himself inside a wonderful new world of many different ornaments, old and new. A beautiful young maiden in a pink dress spun around and danced to the tune that she was singing.

Several animals of different shapes and sizes were running across the floorboards below and a glass ape was climbing the shelving. Each ornament was alive and moving freely, not sat in one place as ornaments usually are, but bursting with energy and excitement. It was as if these creatures had so much energy, as though they had not been alive for a long time.

Bobby rubbed his eyes and looked around even more. This was like another world. As Bobby became oblivious to anything but the amazing scenes in front of him. Dothvera flew to see his brothers and began to speak to them in Shamlen.

"Dos hera," ("He's here") Dothvera Ferrucio said

"Wo e do?" ("Who is he?") one of his brothers replied

"Sothlen ov Calebreh, dos Sera Bobcat granosoth," (Son of keeper, he's sir Bobcat's grandson). The dragons all looked towards Bobby in amazement, they now knew who he was, and one of them knew how important that was.

"Dos menento ecra hera," ("He's meant to be here"). Dothvera Cherama spoke.

If Bobby Bobcat had heard such words about himself, he would not have been so captivated by the scenes in front of him, but by his own future, for Dothvera Cherama knew the earth's desires and when he said the words that mean 'he is meant to be here' that was very important indeed.

Bobby was busy chasing a porcelain frog that was jumping further and further away from him. Dothvera Cherama told his brother to keep an eye on the boy or as he put it, "Caleh o yeeyo ah cra Bolo." which of course would make no sense to you or I, or of course Bobby himself.

Dothvera Ferrucio flew down and received a letter in his mind from his brothers on the way over to the young boy who was still busy playing.

"Bobby, I need to tell you something." Bobby looked up, he realised that in his distraction he had moved quite far away while following the porcelain frog and he was rather surprised by this. He nodded at Dothvera and stopped to listen for a moment.

"My brothers and I have all agreed to take you."

"Take me where?" asked Bobby, "Home?"

"No, Bobby to our fatherland Shamlu. Now your grandfather was a very brave man, very brave indeed, but even he told me that if I ever try this again, that I must warn the person first. So, I am warning you Bobby that we are about to fly straight into that window over there." Bobby looked as Dothvera pointed to the window of the shop and he felt the fear rising inside of him.

"Now, remember that only I possess the magic to get us through this, but..." Bobby looked at the window again and gulped the fear down.

"But others," Dothvera continued, "Others have tried without magic such as mine and have been broken into smithereens." the young boy looked up at the dragon with terror in his eyes.

"Do you understand Bobby?" the boy nodded.

"Listen, while you are riding with me. You possess some of my magic too and that means that you WILL go with me, but you must have faith Bobby, you must believe you can do this or the magic will not work. Do you believe Bobby? *Can* you believe?"

Believe. Bobby knew he had heard that word before. An image came into his mind of when he was a child sitting on the floor watching his mother and grandfather talking between themselves.

"I don't want you putting anymore silly stories into his mind Dad, he's got to grow up!"
"But every boy needs stories Jenny, or they wouldn't survive, let him be a child a little while longer,"

"For goodness sake Robert, he needs to learn something useful, why can't you teach him Maths, or English or something normal?" Jenny cried at the old man sitting in his large leather chair, calm as can be, while she desperately tried to change his mind.

"My dear Jenny." Robert replied calmly, "Your boy is a fine young boy, a fine young boy indeed, and you must have faith that he will grow into a fine young man also." Jenny looked at Robert with a sorrow that even he could not have missed.

"Ever since he's gone I thought I could trust you to care for Bobby somehow, I thought you could become a father to him, to help him with his schooling and instead you're telling him silly stories about Boglets and pirates and all kinds of ridiculous nonsense he's being told not to spend his time on," Jenny said desperately.

"Oh, dear Jenny, if only you could just have a little faith in what you see, you must believe Jenny that everything is exactly as it's meant to be,"

"Believe?" sighed Jenny with frustration, "I have no reason to believe in anything anymore."
Robert put his head down understanding the sorrow his daughter in law was going through, but he knew that his son had only gone into another place, that he was still there watching over the family. If only he could tell Jenny that, but she was so overcome with loss, she could not see the light.

Bobby, then a four-year-old boy, looked up at his grandfather and asked, "Grandpa, what is believe?"

"Aaah my boy," said Bobby's grandfather with a warm twinkle in his eye. "Believe is to bring things to life with your mind." Robert nestled his large, weathered hand into Bobby's soft hair and rustled it gently.

"Do you believe Bobby?" said the dragon looking down at the small young boy before him. He put his head down in front of Bobby, as though to invite him along on the greatest adventure a young boy could ever hope to have. Bobby climbed on and clambered up the neck of the dragon.

The dragons took their places hovering in the air and readying themselves before the window. They then began to chant.

"Enrusha Dothvera, Enrusha Dothvera, Enrusha Dothvera." They called out, getting faster and faster as they said it. Then as they lined up together side by side, they brought up their wings and touched each corner of each other's wing, until they looked like a long line of dragon wings. Then they began their flight.

"Do you believe Bobby?" Dothvera called out.

"Yes," said Bobby firmly.

Closing his eyes for a moment he imagined flying straight through the window and making it out alive. The dragons flew direct. Wings together, heads down, tails up. Bobby opened his eyes and watched as each of their heads disappeared through the window. Still riding Dothvera,

CHAPTER 2

Bobby saw as the dragon's head totally disappeared in front of him. As Bobby came closer and closer to the window, he put his own head down and believed with all his might.

CHAPTER 3

Entering Shamlu

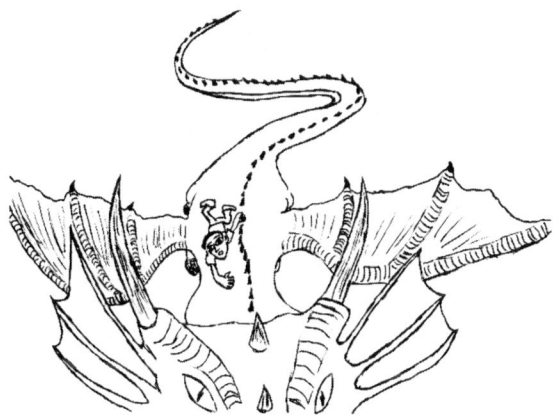

"Head up Bobby, open your eyes!" called Dothvera, "Woooooooooohoooooo"

Dothvera cried out and his brothers followed his calls into the air. Bobby noticed that this world was brand new. He also noticed something else, the dragon's neck no longer felt hard, it was scaly and soft and hairy all at the same time.

"Dothvera?"

"Yes." said the dragon swooping and flying and darting through the air along with his brothers.

"Have you become real?" Dothvera laughed. He sent the message to his brothers and Bobby was shocked when he heard their laughter drifting through the air.

"How did…?"

"WAIT!" Dothvera called, "One question at a time Bobby! And in answer to your first one, yes, I'm reeeeaaalll!" he said spinning himself and Bobby around through the air.

The dragons all seemed to be flying in the same direction, Bobby watched as the floor seemed to appear before him like magic. He couldn't make out everything, but he saw mountains and trees of all shapes and sizes, all hugely different from home, and creatures that he couldn't quite make out in the distance.

As he hung onto Dothvera's neck he began to make out all kinds of magical things. He was sure that he saw fairies dancing along a lake and at one moment a stampede of unicorns (or at least what looked like unicorns) bright white horses too bright to look at in the sunlight and with beautiful horns coming out of their heads, in different colours and patterns. Bobby was sure that this world had it all, all the magical creatures anyone could ever imagine seemed to live here. It didn't make any sense to him, but he liked it. It was mesmerising.

After what felt like a short journey the dragons stopped to rest.

"We're safe here Bobby." Dothvera said as the four dragons flew down to what looked like a huge gap in the earth below. "Safe Haven is the safest place to be, it is a good sleeping place for dragons, especially us four. It's not easy to find a place big enough to rest your head when your head is my size Bobby."

The boy smiled and the dragon lowered his head to the ground and Bobby wandered along his neck and jumped onto the ground below him.

"Dothvera?" asked the boy, so curious about everything around him.
"Yes, my lad," answered the dragon.
"I have so many questions I don't know where to begin,"

"Why not begin at the start, hmm." Dothvera replied, and as the two new friends were talking the other three dragons fell asleep in a circle around them both.

41

"How did you get so real?"

"Well, it might not be easy for you to understand, my boy, but I'll try and explain it. A long time ago, we Dothvera, with the help of someone from your world, built a protective layer around our world for fear that your kind might find it and try to destroy it. This is the world where dreams lay. Shamlu is a world where everything that has ever been imagined goes. The reason why ornaments are so special is because they are the closest thing to reality that can be seen by humans. So they all become real on the edges of Shamlu, especially in the ornament shop for that is where most of the magical ornaments live. That is why Shamlu is such a beautiful place, but it is also a dangerous place. Every fearful and every beautiful thing that has ever been imagined lives here,"

"I used to fear Mick Bushbel but I have a feeling there are worse things than he in Shamlu,"

"What is Mick Bushbel?" Dothvera asked.

"He's a bully. He thinks my name is stupid, I suppose it is rather silly, Bobby Bobcat. He pushes me at school and takes my school bag from me,"

"Well I don't know why you would think your name is silly Bobby. You possess the greatest name in the history of Shamlu! Worlds have heard of you that you have never heard of, and I would never wish to be called anything else other than what you are called now. Never let anyone tell you different, people fear what they don't understand Bobby,"

"It's just, I'm not like everyone else, I'm a bit different," said Bobby holding his head down.

Dothvera lifted the boys chin with his wing.

"Always be proud of who you are Bobby, being different is a good thing. When I first coughed, I coughed fire Bobby. Now that's different,"

"But you, you're magnificent! You are the reason for many stories in our world. You are a dragon. A magnificent dragon!"

"Magnificent? That does sound good." answered Dothvera and yawned a yawn that could have stretched out into the farthest lands it was so loud.

"I'm off to sleep now Bobby, busy days ahead of us, yes?" Bobby nodded as he yawned too, and sleep took him away.

Bobby awoke to the most amazing scene in front of him. Three of the largest creatures he had ever had the chance to meet, were sleeping in a circle around him and he was sleeping on top of one of them.

For what seemed like miles away, there were scales of different colours. Dothvera Ferrucio was a beautiful dark red, and Dothvera Velara, was different shades of bluey green. Dothvera Cherama was greeny brown, and Dothvera Potentioh was what Bobby could only imagine being the colour of a golden sunset.

It was rather magical being as small as the young boy was, even though he was tall for his age. As far as his eyes could see were dragons. Someone who was not so small would not have looked at this in such wonder and amazement. Bobby could make out only colours and lumps and bumps, and small sections where the dragons had curled up their wings. Had he not known these were dragons, he could have mistaken them for mountains and hills.

Bobby took a moment to just sit and stare out at this wondrous view and go back over what he had found out so far. Dothvera's voice came into his mind, "Every fearful and every beautiful thing that has ever been imagined lives here."

"Umm, what was that?" Dothvera's head shook and he mumbled and groaned a little, although it felt like the land itself was shaking and mumbling it was so loud. Bobby jumped up.

"Dothvera?" he said.

"Oh, you're awake, I thought I heard something." 'Heard something?' the boy wondered.

"Yes," answered the dragon, but Bobby was only thinking.

"But I didn't say anything Dothvera,"

"Oh, oh! Ohhhh." Dothvera said gradually making sense of it as he repeated each word. He didn't imagine that the boy might have acquired some powers of his own when entering Shamlu.

"Dothvera?" asked Bobby.

"I think you might have the ability of, well I'm not sure what you'd call it, but we call it tofrero, it's the ability to transfer thoughts to another, but it doesn't seem like you do it all the time Bobby or I would have heard it before. Was there anything different about this time?" Bobby wondered.

"I'm not sure really, I was focusing on the words you told me about Shamlu,"

"Focusing? Yes, that could be it!" said Dothvera.

"Try it again." Bobby closed his eyes and focused entirely on saying something in his mind,

'Dothvera dragons are magnificent' he said in his mind.

"We are, aren't we?" Dothvera answered. The dragon was right. Bobby could transfer thoughts from his mind, but Dothvera Cherama was listening in and warned the boy.

"You must be careful with this power Bobby as it is a power that only someone from your world could possess. People like you are enormously powerful in Shamlu. You are imaginer's, focusers of the powerful mind and you can bring great wonder but also great devastation to our world,"

Dothvera Cherama rarely spoke another's language but he was a wise dragon who had picked up much knowledge over his lifetime. When he needed to say something, he did, and most importantly he could. All of the dragons knew a little of the languages from the manlands.

Shamlu needed it, for without that communication Shamlu could never be safe. So, the Dothveran dragons possessed the ability to speak whatever language they wished when it was absolutely necessary for them to do so.

Bobby began to wonder how much more there was to find out in this new world he was in. He thought back to his own world and felt a sadness wash over him. He had been in Shamlu for quite some time now, and he wondered if his mother was missing him at all. He was missing her.

He feared that if he stayed here too long then she might forget him altogether.

"Careful Bobby," said Dothvera sensing the boy's sadness taking him over, "Be careful of your fears in this world Bobby, it only takes a few moments more and a Boglet could pay you a visit.

"I'm just scared that my mum is out there and I'm here and it's amazing but..."

"Bobby, all I'm saying," continued Dothvera, "...is that the greatest thing to fear in Shamlu is fear itself. Fear is held in your imagination, but so is love and joy and wonder and amazement Bobby, and fear here is the worst thing you can have. Boglets will soon pick up on fear in this world and they will come for you, but you are always in control of that Bobby. Remember a few moments fear is okay, but do not allow it to take over or it will win. If you catch yourself in fear Bobby try to become aware, because Boglets feed on the fear of boys like you."

Bobby nodded and stopped himself from dwelling on his fears that his mother might forget him.

"And trust me Bobby, we will take you back, in time, Dothvera dragons are true to their word,"

"Okay," answered Bobby. The boy had no choice but to trust Dothvera Ferrucio for so far, the dragon had kept him safe and had treated him well. After all Bobby did want to discover more about Shamlu and maybe that was why he was here. He decided that it would be a good distraction to focus on the journey ahead and try to not let the Boglets anywhere near him. They didn't sound very nice at all.

Bobby's mum had told him a similar thing the day his dad had died. She had wiped away his tears and her own and said to him "How about we have a cup of cocoa and watch our favourite film tonight hmm?"

Bobby remembered how the beautiful taste of warm, soothing cocoa was, and the laughter and tears his mum and he had shared watching a Disney film, silenced the upset in his mind for a moment. The distraction was a much-needed moment for them both that day.

The Dothveran dragons were all bringing themselves up on their feet to begin their next flight to their destination. They knew where they were going, and they knew that it wasn't far away to the centre of Shamlu where the home of the dragons, the five towers lay.

"Time to go Bobby," said Dothvera and the boy climbed up and made himself a comfortable seating position and grabbed on tightly to Dothvera's strong and scaley skin.

"Reeeadddy." called Dothvera and Bobby called back, "Yes."

"Woooooooohoooooo," called the dragons as they began to lift and soar up into the skies.

"Dos nad redeilo," ("He's not ready") Dothvera Ferrucio said trying to protect Bobby from what he was about to discover about himself.

"Dothvera Ferrucio, dos alveyah ra redeilo," his brother answered.   Dothvera Ferrucio wasn't quite sure that this young boy had always been ready for this life. Bobby had not had a chance to be trained, he hadn't had a chance to grow into a man that could be prepared for a life in Shamlu. He was only a child, only a boy and Shamlu was a big world for him to become such an important part of.

The dragon watched as the boy slept and he and his brothers discussed his future. He feared for the boy. He felt protective of him, as he had once felt protective of his grandfather. Sir Robert was the greatest Keeper that Dothvera had ever known. He was brave and fearless but kind and loving and calm all at the same time. How could poor Bobby live up to all of that at such a tender age? The boy hardly knew his own world well enough, let alone the world he had fallen into.

Bobby awoke to find himself lying in a bed of fallen unicorn feathers that the dragons had collected from the skies to lay him down upon. He almost felt like he was waking in his own bed. He looked up to see all four dragons talking amongst each other.

"Dothvera?" called Bobby.
"Hello, young lad, you must have felt tiredness come and take you. We have arrived."

"Where are we?" said Bobby rubbing the sleep from his eyes.

"This is the safest place you can be Bobby. This is our home, our horetha. Horetha ov dragero, home of dragons. Bobby just one piece of advice. Don't try to get down from here without one of us, okay?" Bobby looked around and noticed that the stone building they were in was in the clouds, it was so high up. He even wondered if these towers had been built in the clouds themselves. They were so high.

"Bobby, we need to tell you something," said Dothvera Cherama.

"Me?"

"Yes you." Bobby noticed that Dothvera Cherama and Dothvera Ferrucio were standing next to the opened book, that Dothvera Ferrucio had been sitting upon when the boy had first met him.

"In this book is a list of the Keepers of Dothvera Bobby." said Dothvera Ferrucio, "Come closer and take a look,"

Bobby walked up to the large book and climbed up the sides of it. The parchment edges were almost like large steps, and Bobby managed to clamber up them by himself. He walked along the large piece of parchment and came to the name, 'Bobby Bobcat' in golden ink.

Above it was his father's name Daniel Bobcat, and above that was his grandfather's name, Robert J Bobcat. Above that, were all the Bobcats before them. Bobby looked at the names of his father and grandfather, next to his grandfather was the word vethreaah and next to his fathers.

The words were clearly written in magic ink of some kind, Bobby noticed that his name was lit up in a golden light and every name above it was as though it was in a shadow. Still gold, but no longer highlighted.

CHAPTER 3

"What does this mean?" the boy asked Dothvera
Ferrucio.

"It means you are Calebreh Bobby, Keeper of
Dothvera. It means you are especially important
and there is much we have to discuss with you,"

CHAPTER 4

Destiny

Bobby had more questions running through his mind than he had ever asked in his whole lifetime. He didn't quite know if he'd ever answer them all, but he wanted to know so many things.

Meanwhile, the Dothveran Dragons were talking about the young boy's future. Dothvera Ferrucio wasn't sure that Bobby could take on the pressure of being the boy that was meant to save this world. After all, he was only a boy.

"Dos torto yoveroh," ("he's too young") said Dothvera Ferrucio to his brother.

"Dosa nad chosero, iv itt rettero. Do pripamento," ("He has no choice, it is written. Prepare him") replied Cherama.

This time his voice sounding rather forceful, as if he were telling his brother what to do, instead of asking him. Dothvera Cherama knew that Bobby was just a boy, but he was also wise enough to know that even young boys possessed powers that could save this world. The prophecy had been clear, and even though it was a lot for Bobby to take on. It had to be him. He was the only one who had turned up in Shamlu. It had to be him.

Knowing that his oldest brother was the wisest and most respected of all the creatures in Shamlu, Dothvera Ferrucio did as he was told and proceeded to lower his head down in front of Bobby, so that the boy could climb up onto his large scaly neck.

"Come with me," he said quietly.

Dothvera lifted Bobby into the air as he leapt to another tower. There were five towers that reached into the sky where the Dothveran Dragons lived. The middle tower was a meeting place, the four towers surrounding that were the separate homes of the Dothvera. Bobby watched in amazement as he was taken to another tower and Dothvera Ferrucio took him to his new resting place.

"You will stay here from now on." the dragon said, but as he prepared himself to leave the boy, Bobby called out.

"Dothvera?" he said looking into the dragon's eyes.

"We have much to do," said Dothvera Ferrucio with a coldness in his voice that Bobby had not heard the likes of before.

"I have questions," Bobby said.

"They will have to wait Bobby," the dragon replied coldly.

"But why was my name in that book? What did your brother say about me? What are you going to do with me?" Dothvera tried to ignore the boy, but in his heart, he wanted to help him.

"Please Dothvera!" called Bobby loudly. The other dragons heard the boy's desperate calls from across the halls of the great towers and Dothvera Cherama responded. "Take time to answer the boy's questions and then you can begin. He is right. He deserves to have his questions answered."

Dothvera curled up in front of the boy and quietly said, "Begin,"

"Begin?" asked Bobby.

"What question would you like answered first? But be wise Bobby I don't have a long time to answer, so pick your questions wisely." Bobby nodded.

Curiosity swept over him. What was most important to him? Was it getting back home to his mother, or was it finding out about his future? He couldn't choose. He decided to ask a question about each.

"What is the book that my name is in?"

"A very wise question indeed Bobby." smiled Dothvera with a warmth that he had shown before. "The book is The Secrets Of Shamlu, but there are many pages. It is the page that your name was inscribed upon that is most important Bobby, and that is the page of the Keepers of Dothvera, so named for their important work as protectors of Shamlu, both in this world and in the others."

"So, what does that mean?" asked Bobby

"Your grandfather has named you a rightful heir to the secrets of Shamlu. You are destined to be a keeper of Dothvera." Bobby couldn't quite believe what he had heard. *He* was a keeper of Dothvera. *He* was a protector of a magical world. How could *he* protect anything? He was only ten. He couldn't even keep his bedroom tidy. This was all too much. He needed to get back to his mother.

"I need to get back Dothvera. I need to see my mum." Dothvera cast his eyes downwards.

"Dothvera?" asked Bobby, "Please take me home." Dothvera lowered his head in sadness.

"I'm afraid I can't." Bobby looked up at the dragon in anger.

"What do you mean you *can't*? I have to get back to her, I miss her." cried Bobby.

"But you must stay here for now Bobby. You must be trained. You must learn about our world and our language. You must learn how to protect us. I'm sorry." Bobby ran up to the giant beast in front of him and began to hit at him with his hands clenched.

"But you can't let this happen! I have to see my mum!! I have to see my mum!" Bobby cried out.

"Calm down Bobby." Dothvera said desperately trying to soothe the boys mind before something terrible occurred.

But he was too late. Something terrible did happen. A creature jumped up out of nowhere and began to hiss and stare at Bobby. Dothvera raised his head in protection. The creature looked and realising the power of a Dothveran dragon threw something towards Bobby and disappeared just in time to miss the searing heat of Dothvera Ferrucio's protective breath of fire. Bobby walked over to the item that the creature had thrown to him.

"Bobby don't!" Dothvera protested, but the boy in his innocence did not realise what he was about to pick up. He grabbed the photo frame off the floor. It was one he recognised from his home. It had his mother and father in the picture, and him as a baby boy.

Bobby went to touch the image in fondness of the memory of it, and then the image of him in the picture began to disappear. The parents remained but the baby in the middle disappeared until it was gone entirely. Bobby burst into tears and fell to his knees in sorrow.

"That was a Boglet Bobby. You must try not to focus on your fears." Dothvera said to the young boy kindly. He realised how sad that must have made the boy, but he also knew the truth. Bobby's mother would never forget him, and Boglets were simply awful creatures that could make the darkest of fears turn into a real and tangible image. That's why they were the most feared creatures in Shamlu. They knew how to play with the mind, and that was the greatest power of all.

Dothvera lifted Bobby's head.

"Sometimes, although it is not easy Bobby, we have to have faith that things are working out for the best. I hope you can trust me on this my child, but I am not going to stop you from ever going back to your home. I just have a job to do. I must make sure that you are safe. You are the youngest keeper to have ever existed and you need to be trained, just as every keeper needs to be trained, but Bobby I promise you. Your mother will never forget you and by the time you return, she will not even realise that you have been gone."

Dothvera curled his wing around the young boy and Bobby realised that if he were to ever get out of here, he would need to trust this dragon. He would need to trust that his mother would never forget him. Dothvera told Bobby to step aside and he stood up straight, took in a deep breath and proceeded to burn a hole into the magic of the Boglet's nasty creation.

"There." said Dothvera. "That's what I think of fear." he continued. "It does no good Bobby to dwell on fears, especially here. Boglets are a warning. We must teach you to train your mind so that things like this do not happen again. Yes?" the boy nodded. Dothvera was right. With creatures like Boglets around, fear was the worst enemy in the world. Bobby knew it didn't help to be fearful in his own world. Being fearful of Mick Bushbel had made him hide in the toilets during lunchtimes and forget to do his homework because of worrying about seeing the bully in school the next day. Being fearful wasn't a good thing in Bobby's world, but here being fearful was rather dangerous. Who could say what else Boglets had the power to do?

Boglets had been in Shamlu ever since the Dothvera could remember. They were strange and frightening creatures that only appeared wherever fear appeared. The Dothveran dragons knew that although Boglets had never physically hurt anything or anyone, they did have the power to drive humans mad, with their ability to form into being whatever humans feared the most, and place it right in front of their eyes.

Many keepers had lost their minds and some, their lives, after meeting with Boglets. Boglets were a sign that fear was taking over and that it was about to win.

Dothvera Ferrucio was trying not to let himself be concerned, but he could tell that Bobby was going to run into Boglets far more often, if he could not control his fears in this world where imagination was the key to everything.

CHAPTER 5

The book of Shamlu

Dothvera didn't want to waste any time in training Bobby. After all, Boglets were not the only dangerous creatures in Shamlu. If he was going to become the youngest keeper of Dothvera and fulfil his destiny here, he would need to know how to protect himself. Especially now.

Now that he had come face to face with a Boglet, they would know what was going on and would use it to their advantage. After all, the younger someone is, the easier they are to frighten and Boglets knew this for sure. Bobby had to begin his lessons. Then he could keep them away for sure.

"Lesson One: I am going to show you how to deter a Boglet and how to destroy it, but no one has ever had the power of mind to destroy such a creature Bobby. This is why I am here. While I am here you are safer Bobby, because Boglets are powerful creatures, and so far using these methods we have never found out how powerful they are, because we have always managed to keep them far away,"

"Okay," replied Bobby. He wasn't quite sure if he understood, but he also knew that in Shamlu, not everything made complete sense.

"Right. So, the best thing you can do is to avoid feeling fear or allowing it to become more powerful than you. Does that make sense Bobby?"

"I'm not sure," Bobby answered. How could fear take over him?

"Okay Bobby. Do you remember when you got angry with me?" Bobby lowered his head. He'd forgotten how angry he had been before the Boglet had appeared.

"I remember. I'm sorry Dothvera." Bobby said. The dragon smiled.

"No need for apologies Bobby. It wasn't you that got angry that day, it was fear,"

Bobby thought about this for a moment. What did Dothvera mean? Of course it was him that had been angry. He was the one who was feeling fear. This didn't make any sense.

"If it doesn't make any sense Bobby then say so. Yes?" Bobby nodded.

"Well I suppose you must have read my mind. I just don't get it. How can you say that fear did the things that I did?"

"Because fear was in control by that time Bobby, you didn't have your senses, fear did."

"But fear is just an emotion Dothvera. It doesn't have a life of its own,"

Dothvera chuckled gently, "Oh! It does," he said. "Fear is a living thing just like you or me. It moves through you and takes you over if you let it. Just like a Boglet would if you let it. Gosh, even I could make you do something if you let me," continued Dothvera. "This is what I mean by not allowing fear to take you over. Yes, if you must feel it, but only for a moment and do not let it in. Do not let it too close or eventually it will take you over completely, and you will not be able to control yourself at all."

Dothvera seemed to be saying something that made sense now, but Bobby still wondered what exactly the dragon was talking about. Maybe he would find out as time went on and the lessons continued, so he decided that he would listen and see if things started to make sense.

"So, here's something you must learn to do. Try to be aware of when you are feeling dark thoughts Bobby, because Boglets will not go easy on you. Here fear is your greatest enemy. An even greater enemy than Boglets themselves."

"How can I be aware Dothvera? What do you mean?"

"Try to watch over what you are thinking about. If you find yourself dwelling on thoughts that scare you, be sure to stop them in their tracks. If they begin to feel like they are taking over your mind, then try to imagine all your fears drifting away from you. The best thing you can do Bobby is to distract yourself with good things."

"What kind of good things?" the boy asked.
"Any kind of good thing." Bobby thought for a second.

"But what if there are no good things to think about Dothvera?"
"My dear boy. There is always *something* good to think about."

Bobby thought about this and asked himself what good things he could think about when fear tried to attack him. His mind answered him with images of his mother and with images of him flying through the window, and over the mountains and fields, and with images of Dothvera himself. Of course, these were good things he could think about, but how could he do that with a Boglet in front of him? How could he do that when he was angry?

"But Dothvera?"

"Yeeeees?" said the dragon.

"How can I think about nice things if I'm angry?"

"Well, by that time, fear already has you, and this is the final part of the lesson Bobby. If you become angry then a Boglet is very close, and if you see a Boglet the only way to get rid of it is to look it in the eye and think of the happiest thing you can think of. The most fearless moment you have had. If you can do that, then you will destroy it. So, what is the most fearless moment you've ever had?" the dragon enquired.

Bobby went quiet. What was the most fearless moment he had ever had? He wasn't usually a fearless boy, and he had often been afraid of things, but he tried to think what his answer might be. Suddenly he felt very awkward.

"I don't know," he answered quietly. Bobby felt ashamed. He couldn't think of a time he had been fearless. The dragon smiled. "Here's what you must do Bobby. Sit quietly for a moment and take as long as you need. Just ask your mind to come up with a time when you were fearless, a time when you did something you were previously afraid to do. I'm sure that your mind will think of something." the dragon winked.

Bobby sat still and asked his mind for an answer. "When have I been fearless?" he asked inside his mind. At first his mind went silent, but as Bobby kept asking the question, eventually an image came into his mind of a time when he was asked to read out a poem in front of the class. Bobby was scared because he had written about monsters and Boglets and creatures he believed at the time were only found in fairy-tales.

He was about to make up an excuse to go to the toilet when his teacher suddenly called him up in front of the class. Bobby's heart began to pace, and he felt nervous standing in front of his whole class, which happened to include Mick Bushbel.

He gulped and started to read out his poem and kept his head down. Staring at the page he was holding in front of his face, but when he stopped and to his surprise, the teacher clapped and so did the rest of the class. Bobby's poem was put on the wall outside the English rooms after that. Bobby smiled at the thought and so did Dothvera Ferrucio who had happened to listen in to everything Bobby had thought.

"Have you got something?" asked Dothvera.

"I have." smiled Bobby continuing to tell his story to the proud dragon.

"So Dothvera?"

"Yes"

"You said that this destroys Boglets. But if it's never happened before then how do you know?"

"Oh! It did happen, but *I* have never seen it happen, it happened a long time ago. A lady called Amelia Bobcat did it and she wrote about it, so that's how I know."

"Amelia Bobcat? Is she related to me?" asked Bobby.

"Oh yes Bobby she is, and she's very important, but we'll talk more about her later, yes?"

Bobby couldn't believe it. Amelia Bobcat? She had the same surname as him. He had the same surname as her. Who was she?

Dothvera couldn't tell Bobby all about his great grandmother yet. He hadn't even started to train him. He couldn't let the young man's past get to his head. Bobby was a descendant of the Bobcats, and that was an important thing, but the boy couldn't let that distract him from his lessons. He had to learn about Shamlu now and he had to learn quickly. Time was crucial from now on, and

Dothvera knew it. Bobby had to pay attention and he couldn't get distracted.

Bobby's mind began to wonder about Amelia Bobcat. She sounded quite important, but Dothvera had already said that he would teach Bobby about her later on. But *when* was later on? Time didn't seem the same here in Shamlu. It was a bit like a dream, it didn't make any sense but then it also did make a great deal of sense at the same time.

"Dothvera?"

"Yes." said the dragon, as he lifted up the large book and began to prepare it for Bobby's lesson time.

"Is Amelia Bobcat important to Shamlu?" the dragon was amazed. Bobby was already asking questions.

He wondered how long it would be before he would have to answer them. After all, when this young boy began getting curious about things, it was difficult to stop him. Dothvera wondered if maybe telling Bobby now wasn't such a bad idea after all. Maybe not telling him would be worse.

"She's very important Bobby. Now can we get on with our lesson?" Bobby nodded. He decided he would ask more questions later. After all, Amelia

Bobcat shared his name. They must have something in common.

"So, the next lesson we are learning is from the book called 'The Secrets of Shamlu'. A wonderful book all about Shamlu and all that has been discovered about it so far." Dothvera began to read the book. "This book is a book all about the wonders of Shamlu. A world that I have discovered and written about so that I can remember everything I have learned.

Shamlu is a most wondrous place full of incredible and amazing creatures of all kinds. It has actual flying and fire breathing dragons..."

Dothvera smiled to himself, "...and it is full of creatures I have tried to give names that best represent them. I have filled this book with all that I know and all that I have learned and continue to learn. Please keep it safe as there are secrets in this book that could expose Shamlu and all of its wonders to a world that I do not think could ever understand it or keep it protected from my world. Love and best wishes to you..." the dragon stopped. If he said this name, then there would be more questions indeed. So, he decided to continue onwards.

"Hahum," coughed Dothvera and he began again, "The Shamlu map..."

"Wait a minute!" said Bobby, realising the dragon had not finished what he had started.

"What?" asked Dothvera.

"You said, 'love and best wishes to you' and then you stopped. What was after that?"
"Nothing." answered Dothvera.
"Really? But it sounded like..."

"It was nothing." interrupted the dragon.

"But Dothvera?" the boy questioned, and he ran up on top of the pages before the dragon could stop him.

"Woooooow!" Bobby exclaimed reading the name at the bottom of the first page.

"Amelia Bobcat wrote this!?!"
"Yes. But we must get on with reading it." said Dothvera swiftly.
"But who is she? Why are you trying to stop me from hearing about her Dothvera? Who is she?"

Dothvera realised that he didn't really have a choice. He was trying to protect the boy from his own ego. He didn't want Bobby to get high thoughts of himself as a Keeper just because of Amelia, but he had no choice now. Before Dothvera could move on with training he would have to tell this boy who Amelia Bobcat was.

"Okay. Okay." said Dothvera, "Amelia Bobcat is your great grandmother Bobby,"

"Whaaaaat!" cried Bobby. This was amazing.

"...And she was the first person to discover and write about our world Shamlu,"

"She was?" said Bobby. He couldn't believe it. His name was important indeed. He was a Bobcat. He was Bobby Bobcat. This was awesome. Wait until his mum found this out!

"But Bobby this doesn't mean a thing unless you learn what she learned. Amelia was a very important person, and she is highly regarded in Shamlu, but she took her time to learn everything there was to learn about us and about this world. She never forgot that there was always more to learn Bobby, so let's begin our lessons. Yes?" the boy nodded, but there was no doubt that this news had filled him with pride and excitement.

He was Bobby Bobcat. He was a descendant of the first person ever to have put a foot in the world of Shamlu. This was cool.

"So, I'm the great grandson of the person who found Shamlu?" asked Bobby still surprised by what he was hearing.

"Yes indeed, but let's get on, Bobby."
"But how come I never knew? Why didn't my grandfather tell me? Does my mother know? When did this all happen? How did…"

"Bobby Bobcat!" Dothvera Ferrucio said sternly. "This is exactly why I didn't want you to know about this yet! You're not even ready. You haven't trained. You are just a boy, and this is going to take time. If you are not careful Boglets will be around every corner you turn in Shamlu. You *have* to study or you will not be able to do what you are meant to do, if you can't even set your mind to focus on one thing at a time then you will struggle in this world forever."

"What I am meant to *do*?" asked Bobby. Suddenly wondering what the dragon was referring to. Dothvera Ferrucio sighed. He had said too much. Bobby was certainly not ready to discover his true destiny and this was no time to be telling him everything. Somehow the dragon had to convince the boy that training his mind was the most important thing right now. Bobby stared up at the dragon his eyes wider than ever before. His curiosity at its peak.

"Listen Bobby, your great grandmother was incredible and there is much to learn but now is the time to study. You have much to learn before you can understand her story and her journey. It won't make sense to you yet."

Although he didn't want to, Bobby nodded and agreed to listen to Dothvera and what he wanted to teach him. After all, the best way to find out more about his great grandmother was to be on the dragon's side. So, the boy closed his mouth and opened his ears and listened. This was going to be a long day.

CHAPTER 6

Scrambled eggs

"So, Bobby? As you can see this map is split into five different places. The four Dothveran Dragons care for four of those places but one place is forbidden by the Dothveran Dragons and that is?"

Bobby looked desperately into Dothvera's eyes trying to see if he could remember the answer.

"It's Dahkrath Bobby and it is forbidden because...?" the dragon hoped the boy could remember at least this part of the answer.

"Because it's um. It's not very nice,"
"Exactly. And what lives there?"
"Boglets and Binchums and Grinkles."
"And what do they have in common Bobby?" asked Dothvera.
"They follow fear and misery wherever it lies,"

"Spot on Bobby, well done!" Bobby smiled. Dothvera smiled back, but he did hope that Bobby could remember these important facts when the time came for him to be a true keeper of Dothvera. It was one thing learning about Boglets and Grinkles, but it was certainly another coming face to face with them and defeating them.

"So, after lunch I'm going to tell you all about imagining Bobby. How to battle with your mind and not your muscle hmm?" Bobby thought this sounded very interesting. After all he wasn't sure how imagining could work differently in Shamlu, but he knew that Amelia would describe it in the book as best she could. She sounded like a highly intelligent lady indeed.

Bobby wondered how long ago she must have lived, and if there was any information about her back at home in his world. He promised himself he would find out when he returned. Bobby noticed his mind turning to fear momentarily when he thought of home. He did miss his mother and he would be so glad to see her after such a long time away.

As his thoughts turned darker, he remembered Dothvera's words of warning, "the only thing you should fear is fear itself," Bobby recalled. He decided to distract himself quickly before a Boglet could try to get in. He thought about food and realised he hadn't actually eaten anything yet. This was going to be fun. Eating in Shamlu couldn't be like eating at home could it?

Dothvera asked Bobby what he would like for lunch and Bobby replied that he wouldn't mind some scrambled eggs, like his mother used to make them. Dothvera stood up and told Bobby to imagine the food he would like. This was going to be another training session. The dragon was going to show Bobby what was possible in Shamlu.

"Now Bobby. Sit down and close your eyes and imagine. Well let's see what you will need…" thought the dragon carefully. "I've got it!" he said, "Imagine that you're sitting at a table and you have a spoon in your hand, and you are scooping up the scrambled eggs." Bobby looked at Dothvera confused. What on earth was he talking about? How could that help? The boy sat and did what the dragon asked of him. Wondering exactly what was supposed to happen.

"Nothing happened." said Bobby upon opening his eyes.

"Dothvera?" Dothvera looked down at the boy and stared at him.

"Bobby. You can't just do it like that." He had been sitting with one eye open and the other shut wondering what was going to happen and seeing if anything had.

"Close your eyes!" the dragon said loudly, which was much louder than anything else Bobby could have ever heard. After all this was a dragon and when he spoke loudly, mountains shook. Bobby closed his eyes.

"Tightly Bobby. Close them properly." Dothvera said.

"Now. Concentrate Bobby. Imagine that the scrambled eggs are right in front of you." Bobby imagined; he could see scrambled eggs in his mind. He pictured them all around him. He imagined scrambled eggs falling from the sky and then he felt something land on his head.

"Oh no!" called out Dothvera in panic. The sky turned the colour of scrambled eggs and like massive storm clouds the scrambled eggs appeared above them and suddenly big blobs of scrambled egg began to drop from the sky.

Dothvera knew he had to do something. He breathed out fire and created a shield between him and the sky. Then he noticed that the boy was still imagining.

"Open your eyes Bobby!" called Dothvera desperately. Bobby listened. Upon opening his eyes, he couldn't believe what he could see. There was Dothvera above him shielding him from what looked like big pale-yellow pillowy things.

"Oh my! Is that scrambled eggs???" Bobby said. He had never seen the likes of this before. Dothvera called down.

"Imagine blue skies Bobby Quickly!" Bobby couldn't believe that Dothvera could think that he had done this, but not wanting to question the dragon in such a critical moment. He decided to do what he was told and closed his eyes imagining blue skies as much as he could. Bobby listened as the dragon stopped shielding them from the skies.

"AAAHHHHHHH!" the dragon said puffing out a huge blast of smoke in the process. Bobby was amazed. He couldn't have done this could he? He watched as small blobs of burnt scrambled egg floated down around him.

One piece that obviously hadn't been caught in the fire had headed down at speed and splashed on the ground creating a huge mound of scrambled eggs nearby. Bobby picked up some from the top of the mound and tasted it. It *was* scrambled egg. It was warm and buttery and frighteningly big. But it *was* scrambled egg. Bobby couldn't believe it.

As Dothvera caught his breath, he began to watch over the young boy who was sitting on the ground next to a big blob of scrambled egg eating it to his heart's content. Bobby was not like any other imaginer that Dothvera had ever known. He was powerful. He had only been thinking of scrambled eggs for a few moments and it had almost destroyed Shamlu entirely.

No wonder it hadn't taken long for the Boglets to get to the boy. His mind was the most powerful that the dragon had seen. His imagination was astonishing but also incredibly dangerous. If he thought about anything other than what was good, he could surely bring danger to himself and those around him very quickly. Dothvera called his brothers over to the skies and decided to ask their advice.

"Dos pocro." ("He is powerful") said Dothvera to his brothers, "Dos mere pocro an meyo yeey everah." ("He's more powerful than I have ever seen")

As Dothvera Ferrucio described what had happened to his brothers they sighed at first in amazement and then in fear. Bobby had more upon his young shoulders than any keeper had ever had. The dragons weren't sure what to do. He still needed training, but his training would need to be much more about his imagining than anything else. This would soon become his greatest asset.

"Vere nokala dos pocro, nad oin percroh acra enrusha ac dothvera ac egrement ac do." ("We knew he was powerful, not one person has opened a doorway as easily as he") said Dothvera Cherama.

"Nad sencencio Acmemento," ("Not since Amelia"). The dragons gasped.

Amelia was the most powerful imaginer and it had been a very long time since she had gone to Vethreaah. She was so powerful, yet her love and her kindness had kept Shamlu safe for a long time. Amelia had entered this world completely by accident and so had Bobby. They both had the purest of hearts, but Bobby was young and hadn't yet trained himself in the ways of the mind and Amelia, though she was the same, had entered Shamlu a lot later in life. She was a truly amazing person, full of love, courage and kindness.

She had tried to show love to a Boglet and thought of it as a rather unique and piteous creature when it came to her. Although it had tried to bring her fears to light, she showed the Boglet love and found that it had disappeared right in front of her before she had even had the chance to touch it with her kindness.

Bobby and Amelia were truly alike, but Bobby was afraid of this world sometimes and that meant that Shamlu could be a dangerous place. Also, he was easily distracted and that was not a good thing.

If the boy could not learn to focus his mind, he would surely find Shamlu a difficult place to be. Being an imaginer in Shamlu was the hardest thing to be, because here *everything* was imagination. Everything was created by humans. Everything here was imagined by someone in Bobby's world. The good and the bad. Bringing a human into Shamlu could threaten it entirely. In this world where things could be imagined and brought to life almost immediately, controlling the mind was vital. In fact, most Keepers were trained for many years before even being allowed to enter Shamlu.

"Dothvera?" called up Bobby realising that the dragon had been talking to his brothers for some time.
"Yes, my lad." answered Dothvera Ferrucio.

"I'm pretty full now. I don't think I'll need to eat for a while." said Bobby with a big smile on his face, having eaten his bodyweight in scrambled eggs.

"Okay." answered Dothvera.
"So, what's the next lesson?" the boy asked.

CHAPTER 7

With great power comes great responsibility

Dothvera Cherama told the other dragons to leave him and Bobby alone for a moment together. Then the Earth Dragon, who was the oldest of all the dragons, put his head down in front of Bobby and asked the boy to join him for a glide in the skies.

"I know only a little English my boy." said Dothvera Cherama. His voice seemed older and more powerful than Dothvera Ferrucio's. He commanded attention easily whenever he spoke.

"You remind me of someone Bobby. Someone I knew a long time before now." Bobby listened carefully as Dothvera Cherama took him above the clouds and they drifted slowly in the air of Shamlu. It was unlike any skies that Bobby had been in or seen. These skies often changed colour and sometimes the clouds were white and sometimes they were a mixture of colours. As though they had been painted various colours in various places. A cherub flew by and took Bobby by surprise. It reminded him of the magic and beauty that surrounded him here.

"Did you see that?" asked Bobby
"I did, but I need you to pay attention for a moment. Can you do that?" asked Dothvera Cherama.
"Yes." Bobby replied.

"You remind me of your great grandmother Amelia,"
"You knew her?" Bobby said in amazement.

"We all did Bobby. I was the first to see her and after that Dothvera Ferrucio. However, our two other brothers did not know Amelia. Your grandfather created them; they are the youngest Dothveran dragons."

"He did what?" exclaimed the boy in shock.

"He created them with his mind Bobby. Amelia created Dothvera Ferrucio in order to protect us at the time from a rather evil dragon that was causing us all quite a bit of terror."

"So, my grandm..."

"Great Bobby." corrected Dothvera Cherama.
"My great grandmother created your brother?"

"Indeed. A fine example of a caring, kind, considerate yet an incredibly wise and wonderful dragon. That was what she said she wanted him to be and that is exactly what he is."

"So? Who created you?" The dragon smiled at the question.

"I'm not sure Bobby. He or she is in your world. I only know that Amelia created Dothvera Ferrucio because I was there when it happened, and she imagined it right in front of me. Who knows who created the rest of us? That is not important Bobby. But what is important is that you are a great imaginer, and you are just as powerful as your grandmother. That's why you got here without a key,"

"A key?" asked Bobby.

"A key to the heart Bobby, all people from the manlands require a key to get here. They must wear it around their neck and repeat the words to open the doorways. People don't just fall into Shamlu or there would be chaos. You found your way here just like Amelia herself. Quite by accident you see, and your powers resemble hers. This is why you fascinate us."

Bobby came back to the moment and felt the breeze on his face as Dothvera Cherama calmly took him for a gentle ride through the magical skies of Shamlu. He couldn't quite understand why he was so special or why he didn't need a key to Shamlu to get in. He wondered what this meant and if it was good or bad. But it was difficult to know.

"So, Bobby. The only thing I need you to know from here on in is that you are very powerful in Shamlu, and what happened today has shown exactly how powerful. Someone like you could imagine this world away Bobby. Someone like you has the power to destroy good as well as evil. For someone like you it is essential that you focus your mind and be clear about what you want. Try to clear your mind and try not to be so easily distracted Bobby. Shamlu is only the wonderful place it is because of Amelia and how she protected it, and because of your grandfather and the kindness he had seen growing up. A young mind like yours needs training. Every single moment you need to practice imagining until you can use it to your advantage."

Bobby was a bit overwhelmed about what he had just been told. He? A powerful person that could destroy this wonderful, magical world? But he was just Bobby. He wasn't anything special. He was the kid no one really understood at school, and the kid that didn't really understand anyone else. How could *he* have the power to do all that?

"Before you argue with me about this, remember what happened today Bobby. Just ask yourself what would have happened if my brother hadn't protected you and all of us in Shamlu. How could it have ended?"

Bobby thought about it. Even though it seemed absurd at the time to see such a large amount of scrambled eggs. He guessed if he hadn't stopped imagining them then the whole of Shamlu would have been scrambled egg. It sounded crazy. Maybe it was crazy, but then maybe it was also true.

"Sometimes the craziest of things are also the truest." said the dragon before preparing himself to land. When Dothvera Cherama did land, he held his neck to the ground to allow Bobby to jump off him and onto the ground. The dragon looked at the young boy and stretched his neck down to say his final words.

"Remember Bobby. Train your mind. Do not allow it to take over. You must become it's master and make sure that your powers bring light to Shamlu and not destruction."

"Dos redeilo. Nectra elsonah." ("He is ready, next lesson.") Dothvera said to his brother. Dothvera

Ferrucio replied with a loud sound that sounded like "Hmmmmm." or 'yes' and the dragon began to talk to Bobby again.

"So, now our lessons have changed Bobby and we will be teaching you imagining skills first, as it is important that we do not have another situation like yesterday. Is that clear?" asked the dragon.

"Yes Dothvera." nodded Bobby.

"So, I think we must begin with something that cannot destroy all of us. We need to practice creating something that is not scary, and can disappear easily Bobby. Have you any ideas?"

"How about snow Dothvera?" Bobby remembered that snowflakes themselves were exceptionally light and soft things that soon disappeared.
"Ahh yes, but then they would turn into water Bobby and that could cause a problem,"

"But you are a fire breathing dragon Dothvera!" said Bobby shocked that the dragon would see snow as a threat to something like him.

"Yes, I know but I can't dry things quickly. I can only heat them up and set them on fire and that would just create lots of boiling hot water. Oh dear!" The dragon grimaced at the thought. It couldn't be snow. Then Dothvera had an idea. If he could set things on fire, then cardboard was a very good idea for the boy to imagine.

After all, cardboard could be turned into dust and dust was no problem in Shamlu.

"I've got it! Can you imagine cardboard?"

"How about cereal boxes?" said Bobby
"Are they made of cardboard Bobby?" asked Dothvera not knowing what 'cereal boxes' meant.

"Yes." he replied, and the dragon prepared himself for this next lesson.

"Okay Bobby. You know what to do." the dragon said in anticipation. The boy closed his eyes tightly and focused on cereal boxes. Then he opened his eyes a little to check on his progress.

"Oh well." Bobby said, upon noticing that nothing had happened.
"No Bobby. Something went wrong. It happened so easily last time."

The dragon took a moment to collect his thoughts and then realised what had happened. Bobby didn't know his own power before now. Now that he knew it, he had one extra thing to do.

"Bobby. Do you believe that you can create cereal boxes?" Bobby lowered his head. He didn't believe that it was possible to create something with his mind. That was impossible for sure. He hadn't expected any cereal boxes to appear.

"It's impossible Dothvera, I can't do something like that. I'm only…well, me!" Dothvera sighed. He needed to remind this boy how magical a place Shamlu was. He needed to make sure that Bobby trained himself correctly.

"Look Bobby, your mind is getting in the way, do you know that there are other Keepers and they cannot do the things that you have done? Do you know that your great grandmother had these powers too and that's why this book is written? Do you know that she created me? Do you know that you are one of the youngest Keepers and in all my time of training and all our time of training Keepers to protect Shamlu, YOU Bobby. You are the first to have done this? No one else has ever created something so big so quickly. It may have been odd and it may not seem possible to you, but I saw the skies open up and I saw magic like I have not seen before and it came from you Bobby! You must believe this because it just happened and now you can do it again! It's just like when I flew into the window Bobby. You must believe in the magic or it will not exist. Yes?"

Bobby responded by closing his eyes again and imagining cereal boxes as much as he could. He could do this! He was a Bobcat and that meant that he was powerful in Shamlu. He did get to Shamlu very easily. He did create scrambled egg skies very quickly. He was the youngest keeper in this world, and he could do this. Bobby focused on cereal boxes.

All kinds of cardboard cereal boxes falling from the sky. He focused deeply on what that might look like. He closed his eyes tightly and made the cereal boxes so real. He thought of them in detail and what they might look like and what it might feel like to see them all falling from the skies. He started to expect that it might even happen.

"Woooaah, Bobby look!" cried Dothvera. Bobby opened his eyes to a sky full of cereal boxes.

"You did this Bobby. YOU DID IT!" Dothvera cried in excitement. Dothvera got himself ready to destroy the cardboard boxes that were heading towards him. But just as he breathed in, he noticed them all begin to turn into butterflies and fly away in different directions.

Amazed, he turned around to find Bobby behind him. Eyes closed tightly, imagining.

"Woow!" the dragon sighed in wonder. This boy truly was a master of imagination.

Bobby opened his eyes. The plan had worked. He watched as butterflies flew into all corners of Shamlu. One even landed on his nose, stayed for a moment and then fluttered away into the breeze. Bobby was beginning to believe in this magical world he was in. He was also beginning to believe that he could make anything happen here in Shamlu. Anything he wanted. He looked up at Dothvera who was still staring in amazement at the skies.

"How did you do that?" asked Dothvera.

"I believed and closed my eyes and imagined." Bobby answered.

"Yes, but you picked it up so quickly. I was expecting that to take quite some time Bobby."
"Well, I'd like to make sure I can get home in time." said the boy.

Dothvera sat looking proudly at Bobby. He was already growing up into an amazing young man. His grandfather would certainly be proud of him. In fact, anyone that was named Bobcat before him would be proud of him. Dothvera Ferrucio could see great things ahead for this boy and that was a fantastic thing to foresee indeed. Maybe the lessons would go by quickly after all.

"Okay let's try something else!" said Bobby, excited that he had worked out how to conjure anything he wanted.

"How about we make sweets fall out of the sky so that we can collect them? Or ... or, or chocolate bars? Or maybe those lovely little chewy things that look like miniature bears..."

"Bobby." said Dothvera sharply, "This isn't a game. It is important that you remember that you are here to protect Shamlu. We can't get carried away with silly ideas. It is important that we get you trained properly. I think it's time you met the others."

'Others?' thought Bobby. Dothvera heard his thought very clearly.

"Yes, the others," answered the dragon to the young boy's surprise. Bobby then remembered that he could transfer his thoughts to Dothveran dragons. Something he often forgot.

"Oh, I forgot I could do that." said Bobby.
"I know you did." smiled the dragon, as if he had heard a lot more than Bobby had realised.

"What others did you mean Dothvera?" asked Bobby.

"The other Keepers. I will see when we can arrange a meeting. You will need to practice the art of battle Bobby as there may be a great war ahead of us. Play with imagining if you must, but you have to learn how to use this in the face of fear and that may take some time. It is still early days yet, but I think you are ready. I will consult my oldest brother Dothvera Cherama on this matter."

Dothvera Cherama was glad to hear of the boy's progress in imagining the things around him. It would take the boy time to discover all the magical wonders of Shamlu but he had plenty of that while he was here. Dothvera Cherama recalled meeting Amelia Bobcat and how she had accidentally discovered her powers when she was in this world.

Upon meeting the dragon, she had created a large shield in front of herself out of fear that she would be eaten or something worse. She was amazed when she had looked up and realised the dragon had been replaced by something she had wished for in her mind. A large shield. Dothvera Cherama was taken aback also.

Having never met a human before, he did not realise that Amelia could do such things and together they tried to learn each other's languages and discover more about each other's worlds. They had become awfully close friends. Dothvera remembered the last time Amelia had seen him.

She looked hugely different to how he had remembered her. She had become old and frail and although the light still shone in her eyes, she could no longer do the things she had done before. She named the person who she wished to take on her responsibilities as a Keeper, said her goodbyes, and had never returned to Shamlu. Dothvera Cherama still missed her deeply, but he was reminded of her every time he saw Bobby.

The two dragon brothers decided that it was time for Bobby to meet the other keepers. They decided to send out a call to each of their corresponding keepers and to bring them to Shamlu for extra training time. When Bobby found out that the other keepers were going to meet him and he was going to meet them, he wasn't quite sure what to think. Would the other keepers like him? Would they know who his grandfather was? Would they know who Amelia was? What would they be like? Bobby wondered if they would accept him as a fellow keeper as he was so young. He was deep in thought when Dothvera interrupted him.

"What's that mind of yours up to young lad?" asked the dragon kindly.

"My mind?" asked Bobby.

"Yes. That mind of yours Bobby. What's it up to, eh?" Bobby didn't quite know why Dothvera spoke of his mind as a separate thing from him. His mind was *his* mind. It was part of him wasn't it?

"Dothvera?" asked the boy.

"Yeeeees."

"What if they don't like me Dothvera? I mean, what if they think that...?" Dothvera interrupted.

"Now Bobby, remember your training. What do these thoughts sound like, hmm?"

Bobby wondered what exactly Dothvera was asking of him. The thoughts sounded like thoughts.

"I don't know what you mean Dothvera." he answered.

"They sound like something you need to keep an eye on to me. Have a listen. What do these thoughts sound like Bobby?" the dragon enquired. Bobby still wondered what Dothvera wanted from him.

"I don't know." said Bobby putting his head down in shame.

"Lift your head up Bobby, don't let this thing bring you down. Remember what happened before." Dothvera was giving his young friend a clue. He knew the power of Bobby's mind and he wanted to make sure that Bobby could recognise when fear was trying to speak to him.

From now on, this had to be Bobby's job. He had to learn how to spot the signs of fear and stop his mind from attracting all kinds of Boglets. Dothvera Ferrucio had seen what Boglets could do. Those creatures had helped create every fearful thing in Shamlu. They collected dark and deep fearful thoughts and they created awful beasts with this fear. One of the biggest and scariest of those creations Dothvera Ferrucio himself had tried to fight and had eventually beaten, with Amelia's help.

Now that Shamlu was at peace, this world was much less scary but the Boglets were still powerful amongst the weak minded, and some Keepers could be weak minded and had been weak minded, almost releasing the curse a second time around.

Thankfully with the dragons training, many keepers had survived their thoughts and become stronger in the face of the Boglets. Young Bobby had to learn to do the same. But Dothvera had hope. He knew there was always hope in the face of danger.

Amelia had taught Dothvera hope and faith. She somehow knew how to find them both in the most chaotic of situations. Amelia was one of a kind. She still influenced Shamlu and many of the creatures that lived there. She was the first protector and the first of her kind to ever enter the world and she had done wonderful things there with her power. She had separated good and evil and made Shamlu the most beautiful and peaceful place where the Dothveran dragons could soar the skies without fear. Fear itself had been banished from Shamlu and that had changed the world entirely.

"Is it fear Dothvera?" asked Bobby, having spent some time to think on his answer.

"Indeed." answered the dragon proudly.
"Oh." said Bobby putting his head down.

"Bobby." said Dothvera lifting the boy's chin with the tip of his wing. "What is wrong?"

"I got it wrong. I didn't know the answer Dothvera." Dothvera smiled.

"Of course you knew the answer Bobby, but you were distracted by fear and it's okay to be distracted by fear, as long as you do not allow it to take over. And it hasn't taken over Bobby. Well done!"

Bobby realised that Dothvera was proud of him and smiled. Dothvera noticing this, gave the boy some extra wisdom.

"Bobby. You know I am proud of you. Yes?"
"Yes." smiled Bobby.

"However, it would do you good to remind yourself to be proud of you too. You are doing a great job Bobby. Just because there is always something new to learn, it does not mean that you are not learning great things. You are growing all the time. You are always growing Bobby like the largest of trees. You will always be growing and changing with the seasons. Always be proud when you are learning Bobby. Learning is a great thing and never be afraid to get things wrong. Humans are strange about getting things wrong Bobby. They call it failure and they have great fear of failure. But I think getting things wrong is one of the quickest ways to getting things right. If you do not learn how not to do things, you can certainly never learn how *to* do them."

Bobby nodded. Dothvera Ferrucio seemed to be a wise and kind dragon. He seemed to know a lot about humans and their ways. Much like Bobby's grandfather. He seemed to know what to say to make Bobby feel better. Bobby liked that. It reminded him of one of the most wonderful men he had ever known. Robert J Bobcat.

CHAPTER 8

The keepers of Dothvera

The three keepers stood in front of the young boy wondering what to say. It was the first time that they had met this new keeper and they were hoping to have seen someone a bit taller and maybe a bit stronger in front of them. Someone who could put up a fight.

They'd all heard the prophecies about there being a keeper that could avoid the darkest Boglets and would bring an end to the dark war that was ahead of them all, but this was just a child. He was tall for his age maybe, but not quite tall enough. He didn't seem the type of child that could have the strength to face such a battle.

"Um... Hello?" said Bobby nervously.

Standing in a line in front of him were three rather strapping individuals. Totomal, a middle-aged man who was extremely muscular and well trained in the martial arts. Hakramen, a slightly younger woman wearing her battle armour and who could handle a sword better than any man she knew, and Reikiila, the oldest of the group, who looked like he was much fitter than Bobby, were all stood in front of the boy.

They were standing rather awkwardly, staring at him which Bobby found very intimidating. Dothvera Cherama whispered something in Shamlen to his brother Ferrucio and they backed away from the four keepers as if to give them all time to get to know each other. Poor Bobby hoped someone would answer him soon.

The young woman spoke first.

"Hi." said Hakramen "What is your name?"

"Bobby." answered the boy, "And yours?" he replied.

"Here, I am Hakramen. It means strong sword."

"Oh, I see. What do they call you in our world?"

"They used to call me Clara." she replied.

The man on the left of Hakramen stepped forward and shook Bobby's hand firmly. "I am Totomal, it means swift and silent." Totomal bowed to Bobby and the boy bowed in return.

The other man stood back for a moment. So, Bobby stepped closer to him and looked up.

"Who are you?" asked the boy gently. Reikiila, the last man to speak stared at Bobby and studied him before answering quietly. "I am Reikiila. It means intense and wise." he said before returning to his original stance.

Bobby wasn't quite sure why the three keepers had such strange names, but he was definitely going to ask Dothvera about it as soon as he was back in training.

"So, what is your power Bobby?" asked Reikiila, as if to put the child on the spot.

"Umm. Well, I uh,"

"You... uh what?" asked Reikiila a second time.

"I..."

"No need to talk about that now Bobby." interrupted Hakramen, "What do you like to do back home Bobby? How about you tell us that?" Bobby nodded, noticing Reikiila still glaring at him with his piercing and fiercely intimidating eyes.

"I like to draw." answered Bobby. Reikiila sniggered.
"Hey!" Hakramen yelled at him. "Keep yourself to yourself if you don't like the boy, but don't act like a school bully." upon hearing this, Bobby decided to speak up for himself.

"My power is my mind and my magic!" he said to the three keepers, "I got here by accident and I didn't even know you all existed until I got here without a key!" the keepers went quiet.

"Did you say... without a key?" asked Reikiila.
"Yes."

"You weren't shown the doorways??" Hakramen asked.
"No." answered the boy.

"How did you get in then?" asked Totomal.
"I don't know." answered Bobby.

The Keepers seemed amazed. The boy didn't know how he had found his way to Shamlu. Each of *them* had been introduced to this place, trained in the ways of this place. Each of them had been handed a key and had been taught how to say the passwords. Each of them had been trained to enter this world. How could this boy have done such a thing without such training and without a key?

"It's impossible!" yelled Reikiila, "It must be a lie, surely his father would have..."
"My father's dead!" called out Bobby. The three keepers went silent once again.

"Reikiila! Apologise!" said Hakramen to her fellow Keeper. Reikiila ignored her.

"I don't like it one bit! This ridiculous world tries to get certain people to elevate their positions. I mean, a woman keeper was a ridiculous idea and thank goodness you have shown me your strengths Hakramen but... but a boy! A young flimsy little boy! It's outrageous. Look at him!"

Dothvera Ferrucio who had hearing that was beyond what any human could imagine, flew down to face Reikiila immediately. The man stood in front of the dragon and knelt before him.

"You have something to say?!" he roared.
"No your highness, I simply..."
"You simply chose to bully a child that has accidentally fallen into a world he does not know,

that has no father, has recently lost his grandfather and has been pulled from his mother by the magic of Shamlu and you… you dare to speak to him like this." Reikiila lowered his head.

"It would be good for you to remind yourself of how you were when you first came here Reikiila. Your name reminds us of your strengths, but I will strip it from you if you demolish them by bringing us your weaknesses only."

Bobby had never seen Dothvera Ferrucio speak so grandly and so powerfully before. He felt rather proud that he knew this powerful dragon so well, and to have heard him stand up to Reikiila on his behalf was amazing. Dothvera Ferrucio truly was wise, kind and courageous. He was also someone who was not to be messed with. Reikiila stood back and apologised to Bobby. Dothvera decided to increase everyone's respect for the boy by showing them the truth.

"I am sure you are all wondering how Bobby can help us. Well I will tell you how he can help us but first it is time to give him his name. I name him Pocromethrah. It means..."

"Powerful mind." said Hakramen turning to look at Bobby.

"Yes Hakramen. Bobby has one of the most powerful minds I have ever seen. The last time I knew a mind as powerful was Acmemento."

Hakramen smiled a wonderful smile. Acmemento or Amelia was one of Hakramen's inspirations. She was a woman with a wonderful and powerful way about her. However, Hakramen's mind was not as strong as Acmemento's. She knew that her strengths lay elsewhere and the moment she picked up a Shamlen sword, she had focused her mind on becoming the greatest sword fighter Shamlu had ever known and she had succeeded. She had fought Boglets using her special Shamlen sword that the dragons had created for her using magic stone that was created for its powers in defeating dark forces.

The dragon said one final thing before he left that shocked Bobby.

"In a few hours, Pocromethrah will show you the extent of his powers and he will show you what his mind can do, but until then speak amongst yourselves. I need to speak with him. Pocromethrah?" said the dragon placing his head down for Bobby to climb on, "come." Bobby climbed up the dragon's neck and Dothvera Ferrucio lifted his head up and prepared himself to fly into the Shamlen skies.

"It's a disgrace." said Reikiila as the dragon took to the skies.

"I don't think you can speak until you have seen what he can do Reikiila." said Totomal, who wasn't sure what to think about the child but also trusted in Dothvera Ferrucio and his wisdom.

"I think we should trust Shamlu if it has chosen him to enter without permission." said Hakramen, who had taken to the boy. She had found herself in a difficult situation with Reikiila when she first entered Shamlu. A girl, aged twenty-six. Only a child in her mind at the time. Trained but also nervous of the responsibility of being a Keeper of Dothvera. He had used that fear of hers to make her feel small and it had been Bobby's grandfather who had made her feel welcome and taught her to find her powers in this world. Bobby's grandfather who was introduced to Hakramen as Granfairdd ov Dothvera, which meant "Grandfather of Dothvera" who she had always called Granfairdd. She had always been close to Granfairdd. He had shown the woman her powers and had really changed her life.

Now back at the towers in training, Dothvera said "So, what I'm going to need you to do is transform something in front of their eyes."

"In front of who's eyes?" replied the boy.

"The keepers, Bobby. You need to show them what you can do and then they can begin to call you your new name Pocromethrah and believe that it is true"

"It's a bit long though." said Bobby.

"What is?"

"My name Dothvera. Why can't I just be Bobby?"

"You will still be Bobby, but you need a name to call yourself if you are at war. The Dothvera Keepers always use their name to remind them of their strengths. You need to remind yourself who you truly are Bobby and that is a powerful mind. It's not your actual name, just a name we call you to remind you who you are."

"But can't I just be Bobby?" asked the boy.

"I will call you Bobby until you are ready to be Pocromethrah." the dragon said, realising that the boy didn't quite understand the reason for him having this new name.

It was something that Amelia had thought of in order to keep the Keepers secrets safe. She could speak to her friends about important things using their names and only they would know what she had meant. The Keepers had different lives and a different world to live in and depended upon secrets to survive in this world and in their own.

It was what people thought that also scared Bobby. What if he couldn't do this thing he had prepared? What if he wasn't as powerful as his new name was saying? What if Reikiila laughed at him?

"Bobby be careful, or you won't be able to do this." said Dothvera, having sensed the boy's thoughts. Even though the boy was unaware of his abilities, Dothvera knew only too well that a mind like Bobby's was stronger than anything in Shamlu. He had to watch the boys fears closely and ensure that he did not fall prey to his mind. Amelia had fallen prey to her mind only once and he had seen the destruction that it had almost caused right before the war between he and the darkest evil. Bobby needed to watch himself and Dothvera had to watch over that.

"So, Bobby. Let's concentrate on our task. Seeing as I do not have hands. Place the paper into my wings via your mind and then open up the paper into a butterfly, okay?" said Dothvera placing his wings outstretched in front of him.
"Okay." sighed Bobby, closing his eyes.
"Right then. Open your eyes. You're not ready yet."
"What?" asked Bobby who had been preparing himself for the creation.

"You still have a problem with believing Bobby. Pocromethrah is powerful and he will win over others with his ability to astonish their eyes. He will make them believe the unbelievable. He will give them faith that the impossible is possible. His friends will call him Pocro mostly for in their eyes he is simply 'powerful'. Don't you see Bobby? This is who you become. There is no room for disbelief."

Bobby realised that Dothvera was right. How could anyone believe in someone that did not believe in themself? Bobby wasn't sure how, but he had to find a way to bring himself to believe that he was powerful. In this world he was. In this world he had done incredible things. In this world his mind could do almost anything.

"It CAN do ANYTHING you ask!" exclaimed the dragon, reaching into Bobby's mind. Bobby jumped back in surprise. The dragon had spoken to him inside his own head.
"How did you do that?!" asked Bobby.
"There are things I have been given by Acmenento that even I do not know about." said Dothvera.

How true this was.

Amelia had created the dragon to possess powers that far outreached anything she could offer. When she had created Dothvera Ferrucio, she made a rule bound by magic that only a true descendant of hers could ride the dragon or could communicate with him. Amelia knew the powers of Dothvera Ferrucio and his abilities were always growing as she had predicted.

Bobby listened to his mind for a moment and heard it trying to make him afraid. He was afraid sometimes. He was afraid of how long he had been away from his mum. He was afraid that if he couldn't perform this trick for the Keepers, they wouldn't help him to get back home. He was afraid that he wasn't good enough or strong enough to believe in himself and make everyone else believe in him. As Bobby became aware of his fears he thought maybe the best thing to do was to ask for Dothvera's advice.

"Dothvera?" the boy said.
"Yes, my lad."
"How do I stop my mind from being afraid?" asked Bobby. Dothvera felt proud. Finally, the boy was taking his tasks seriously and paying attention.

"I'm glad you asked me that question Bobby, from what I recall Amelia Bobcat wrote something in her journal which I believe is the second book that I am the guardian of. We can take a look if you like."
Bobby nodded. It seemed like the best way to learn how to use this 'powerful mind' of his was to learn from his great grandmother.

Dothvera lifted his feet and clasped around the edges of one book to heave it up and lift it away from the other. Underneath the secrets of Shamlu was a second book with the words 'Acmenento' inscribed in golden ink in the front of its glorious leather book cover.

The dragon uttered the words "Acmenento, Enrusha" and the book unlocked itself and spun open. Then Dothvera Ferrucio said again "Acmenento, Trettorah ov Methrah," the book then flipped its own pages causing a rush of wind that almost knocked young Bobby off his feet. He wasn't expecting what was happening from one moment to the next.

Finally, Dothvera Ferrucio said "Acmenento, English!" and in front of Dothvera and Bobby the books ink changed from the Shamlen to the English language. Bobby who was rather confused and bewildered by seeing such magic called up to the dragon.

"What did you say Dothvera?" asked the boy
"I asked the book to open then I asked it to take us to the right page, 'the teachings of the mind' and then I asked it to translate itself into your language Bobby so that you can read it." Bobby couldn't believe it. Before he asked again, Dothvera told him of the magic that he had just seen.

"It's Dragon's Ink Bobby. A creation of your grandmother's. She was wise indeed. It is magical and it has many wonderful properties. It is unavailable to the eye in any other world but Shamlu. It can transform into any language from any world or time. It will never run out. It can listen to Shamlen instruction and if written in a certain way, it can create anything desired in Shamlu."

"What do you mean? Written in a certain way?"
"It is a secret Bobby. Even I do not know. Your grandmother did not want anyone getting hold of her formula, so she hid it inside her own mind."

"Dragon's ink sounds amazing!" said Bobby, still mesmerised by what this ink could do.
"Yes, but let's see what it says shall we?" said Dothvera, scooping the boy up in his wing and placing him on top of the large book."

CHAPTER 9

Butterflies and Black dragons

"Read it aloud Bobby." Bobby walked along the page as he read the words in Amelia's journal.

"Anyone who possesses a powerful mind must be aware that it is a magical thing in Shamlu. This world responds to the mind in a most magical way. It is something that I have learned much about and continue to learn about every day. Powerful minds must be controlled in Shamlu. I have had much more trouble in this place and much more amazement in this place than my friends. Jegreaath has seen the trouble my mind brings and often asks me what I can do to control it. The key, I believe, is that I do not allow my mind to control me. Often, I find myself in places of fear and I struggle to get past it..." Bobby stopped. He looked up at the dragon. "Is there a way to ask the book to bring up all the lessons on fear?"

116

"Absolutely Bobby," the dragon nodded. Just as he was about to ask, he decided to give Bobby a chance to see what Dragons Ink could do. "Why don't you ask the book Bobby? Its name is Acmemento and the word fear in Shamlen is desstruccio. I tell you what, I shall whisper the words into your mind and you can say them for me, yes?" Bobby nodded. This sounded like great fun.

"Acmenento, Decouver desstruccio" the boy said, repeating what the dragon had whispered to him. The ink in the book disappeared from the page and re-appeared in front of Bobby and Dothvera Ferrucio, the word fear was lit up as if a golden highlighter pen had drawn over the word wherever it appeared in the book. Bobby began to read the sentences aloud.

"Fear is the most terrifying thing in Shamlu. I felt fear and the creature appeared like a dark shadow. Fear almost killed my friends. I am more afraid of fear here than anything else in this world. Dothvera Cherama is nothing to be fearful of. Dothvera Ferrucio will soothe all fears in us. The Black Dragon is the most fearful creature I have ever set eyes on. Fear can be destroyed with love." Bobby stopped.

He re-read the sentence, "Fear can be destroyed with love." Now Bobby knew what he was looking for. "Acmenento," the boy said to the dragons surprise, "desstrucio a lomoraah" Bobby said automatically, not thinking about what he had just done. Dothvera looked on in amazement.

The ink transformed once again and answered Bobby's request. Bobby read the words that appeared.

"Fear and Love are opposite forces, and it appears that in Shamlu to show something fearful love or kindness destroys it. The hardest thing to do is to show true love to something you fear. Facing your fear in the eye and feeling kindness for it, even though it feels only hate for you is possibly the hardest thing I have had to learn to do. Your mind will fight you. You will not do this without practice. I have only learnt of this by accidentally feeling love and wonder when I saw a Boglet, not realising it feeds on fear itself. Since, I have struggled to destroy any Boglets, as I know what they foretell. My fear has become me and this frightens me the most."

Bobby stopped to take in what he had read. Through his mind a picture of his journey so far came alive in his head and he watched as he saw everything that had happened so far. From meeting Dothvera Ferrucio to the moment he had entered Shamlu. From seeing all the ornaments alive in the shop to meeting a Boglet face to face. Bobby was beginning to realise that this world wasn't just a dream world. He wasn't in some strange place. This was a place that Amelia had entered and had explored herself. It was a place with a history and a story of its own. It was more than just a game that Bobby had played in the playground. Shamlu was real and it was here and so was Bobby's power.

Without the dragon noticing, Bobby imagined and brought a large piece of paper next to the dragon. It folded itself into a Phoenix and flew up to Dothvera Ferrucio and to his surprise burst into flames right in front of him and what appeared to be the same piece of paper landed on the floor at the dragon's foot. Dothvera Ferrucio smiled in wonder at what the boy had just done. He was beginning to realise his power and that was vital. Once Bobby knew how to create here, he could devise his own way home and actually create the way himself.

"I see you've found your power Bobby. I think it is a great thing to realise your own power, but I also know that with great power comes great responsibility. You must learn to use your power wisely and not let it control you. Power and wisdom go together. Amelia has a lot more to teach you about Shamlu and about being an imaginer, Bobby. You still have much to learn, but I am glad that you have come so far, so quickly. So, do you think you are ready to show the Keepers what you can do?"

"Of course," answered Bobby swiftly.

"Then we will train some more and make sure that you are doubly confident."

Bobby nodded. He didn't know why Dothvera Ferrucio wanted him to work so hard though. He was great at this mind thing. He knew what to do.

"Then it won't matter if you show me it again, will it?" said Dothvera, reaching into Bobby's mind once again. The dragon did not want the boy to become too confident too quickly or he could find that fear itself would put a stop to his confidence altogether. Confidence in oneself had to be earned and brought in step by step. Yes, confidence was good, but too much of it and fear would soon discover and control you.

Dothvera Ferrucio recalled a time when Amelia was so confident that she could win. She was so sure that her creation of this wonderful dragon would destroy the Black Dragon that she forgot to test her creation out. Instead she started a war that she could not win alone. The next time around, she took time to build up defences. She spent time creating and building magic that could not be destroyed. She was patient and gradually built a force strong enough to bring peace to Shamlu once and for all. Amelia had learned the hard way that being too confident was not always a good thing.

"Learning is valuable Bobby. It is an important skill to be someone that can always learn something new. You need to realise that there is always more to learn and more to become. I feel like sometimes you are afraid that you do not have all the answers all of the time, but, my son, learning is the greatest thing you can do. Your grandfather was a keen student and he always sought to learn more, for he knew that he could never know everything there was to know. He wanted to keep learning and never stop and something that I have learned along the way Bobby is that keen students are the best teachers of all. For they usually know more, but what is great about them is that no matter how much they know, they are wise enough to realise that there is always another wonderful lesson around the corner. Be a keen student Bobby and it will never let you down."

Bobby looked at Dothvera and stood ready to imagine his next magical display. He conjured a piece of paper in his mind and conjured a pen that wrote the words 'Dothvera Ferrucio' and then he conjured a dragon that looked exactly the same as Dothvera himself and it stood in front of him. At first the dragon stepped back in shock and momentarily seemed afraid. Upon noticing this, Bobby made the imaginary dragon disappear and called up to the dragon, who was still a little taken aback.

"Dothvera?!" called the boy. Dothvera looked down at Bobby.

"Are you okay?" he asked.

"Yes, I am Bobby. I just... It just reminded me of something. That's all. Nothing to worry about, but can we try to stick to butterflies for now?" the dragon requested.

"Yes, we can Dothvera." Bobby answered, realising he had scared the largest thing he had ever met, with a mirror image of itself. Bobby wondered why the dragon had jumped back so quickly and what exactly could have caused such a memory for him, but not wanting to upset Dothvera he continued with his practices and decided to find out another time.

Dothvera Ferrucio watched as the boy showed him the creation again. By now, Bobby was turning paper into butterflies with a flicker of his eyelids, but Dothvera asked him to do it again still. Bobby was beginning to wonder what exactly the dragon wanted from him.

"But I just did it Dothvera!" protested the boy.

"And?" asked the dragon.

"Well what exactly do you need from me?"

"I need you to do this in front of Reikiila and the others. You must be so good at it and know that you're so good at it, that not even the fear of getting it wrong will make you go wrong."

"But I can do it Dothvera. I've shown you a hundred times." moaned Bobby.

"Not quite one hundred Bobby. I'm counting sixty two times so far and I know you can do it. I don't need you to be able to do this Bobby. I know you can. I need you to believe that you can do it NO MATTER WHAT." roared the dragon in his final few words. Bobby jumped back in surprise.

Bobby knew that Dothvera Ferrucio could sometimes be quite scary, but he didn't understand why the dragon was so intent on him repeating the same lesson over and over again.

"The more you do this Bobby..." continued Dothvera, "the better you will become. But the key to this whole thing is believing you can do it. If you don't believe then the magic will fail, and you don't want that to happen in front of any of the Keepers. Especially Reikiila, he is the most pessimistic of them all. He has reason to be, but all I can say is you will need to prove yourself. Now no more moaning. It's time to practice."

Bobby's mind was starting to get more and more tired the more he repeated the imagining of the paper into butterflies trick that he was now sure he had learned. Dothvera sensed this and decided it was time to give Bobby a break from imagining.

123

He was Pocromethrah and there was no doubt about it, but even a powerful mind like Bobby's would need to have breaks. As Bobby started his mind up again thinking of what he wanted to conjure up in front of him, Dothvera put his wing up and stopped the boy before he could continue.

"That's enough now Bobby. You have outdone yourself today and I am very proud of how much you have done. Now you will need some time to relax before your big reveal today."

Bobby knew that Dothvera Ferrucio was expecting him to do this for all the Keepers and even though he had turned paper into butterflies time and time again and even turned the butterflies back into paper as well, he was nervous. He worried that with Reikiila watching him he would fail. One day in school with Mick Bushbel watching, Bobby had read out loud and forgotten how to read at one point because he heard the bully sniggering behind him. This time he knew he had to focus but he didn't know how to.

"Dothvera?" asked Bobby.
"Yes, my boy," replied the dragon
"Why are people sometimes mean?"
"Well it depends. I think I was speaking to your grandfather about it once and he said that sometimes people are mean because they are

afraid, and it makes them feel big and unafraid for a while."

"Really?" asked the boy.

"Yes Bobby. Remember when you got afraid of missing your mum and you got angry with me?"

The dragon had made some sense actually. Being afraid was a really scary thing to face. It sometimes made him feel angry too.

"Dothvera? Will I ever get back home?" asked Bobby, not sure whether the dragon had forgotten about Bobby's family and his mum back home.

"I have no doubt in you Bobby. Pocromethrah will find a way home and it will be at the perfect time, I am sure,"

Bobby smiled and tried not to think on the subject any longer in case another Boglet appeared. Thinking about Boglets suddenly another question arose in Bobby's mind.

"Dothvera? What are Binchums and Gr-on-k...?" said the boy trying to remember the word.

"Grinkles I think you are meaning to say Bobby, well Grinkles are in the sea of stench. Awful creatures they are. They look like a huge lump of mud and hair and they rise up from the sea of stench and are not very nice creatures. They try to grab anything they see and drag it into the sea of stench with them. I only recall seeing a few of them and it wasn't a very pretty sight. Mind you,

you can smell them first of all, but they don't live here anymore Bobby." The dragon said, noticing the boy's face crinkle up in disgust at the thought of a Grinkle.

"Binchums, however, are very sneaky creatures indeed. Thankfully they have also been banished to Dahkrath. It is where all fearful things have gone since the 'Wail wit Dragonera Dacra', the war with the black dragon,"

"The Black Dragon?" asked Bobby. He had seen that written in Amelia's journal and wanted to know more. What was this Black Dragon that everyone feared so much? Why was he so scary and what kind of war was this?

"Dothvera? What is the Black Dragon?" Dothvera wasn't sure how much he wanted to tell Bobby about the Black Dragon. He didn't want to put fear unnecessarily into Bobby's mind. But then, this boy was a curious boy and for good reason. He had plenty of reason to question this world he was in. But Dothvera knew he had to use wise words for this one.

"Bobby. The Black Dragon was a darkness that used to be in Shamlu, but it has gone now and good has finally won over evil here. For now, there is no Black Dragon. He is in Dahkrath. He was banished a long time ago. You do not have to think about him. Try to focus on your own task ahead. Shall we go and show the Keepers what Pocromethrah can do?"

Bobby nodded but he still wasn't sure. Could he do this?

CHAPTER 10

The birth of Pocromethrah

The smile on Reikiila's face put an extra dash of fear into Bobby's mind when Dothvera placed him down in front of the Keepers for the second time. Totomal and Hakramen looked curious but Reikiila looked like a cat that had just got the cream, as if Bobby was only going to look stupid in front of everyone and he would be revealed as a fool after all.

Mick Bushbel's face came to mind for Bobby and Dothvera, who could sense this placed the tip of his gloriously large wing on Bobby's shoulder and spoke proudly to the crowd. The three Keepers and their dragons standing behind them watched like an eager audience as Bobby standing small and feeling slightly intimidated listened to Dothvera's wise words.

"Everyone. I would like you to remind yourselves that although Shamlu is a peaceful home to many wonderful creatures. It is also home to many scary and nightmarish creatures. The power that brought peace to our home was through Acmenento's mind. It changed our world into a place where we could play and enjoy life without torment. The Dothveran Dragon's believe that Bobby Bobcat, who is a true descendant of Amelia Bobcat and grandson to the fantastic and wonderful Robert J Bobcat, standing before you, is just as powerful and possibly more powerful than his ancestors. This is why we believe his Shamlen name to be 'Pocromethrah' but first he will show you why that name is so well deserved."

Bobby gulped. This was such a big introduction. He looked up at the three wondrous dragons all waiting to see what he could do. Reikiila was still grinning slyly at him. Bobby wasn't sure he could really do this now.

He turned to Dothvera Ferrucio with fear in his eyes and whispered to the dragon in his mind, "Dothvera what if I can't?" and Dothvera looked deep into the boys eyes with his huge expressive golden eyes as he transferred a message back to Bobby, "Oh but my boy. What if you CAN?"

Suddenly from behind Bobby a voice spoke up.

"This is lovely and all that, but I thought we were going to have a show." Reikiila said loudly, trying to make a point.

"I mean what kind of show is this? This is ridiculous!"

"ENOUGH!" shouted Dothvera Ferrucio pounding his front foot forward into the ground and lowering his head until it was right in front of Reikiila's. "YOU DARE TO TEST MY KEEPER?" Reikiila shook with fear at the dragon's unwavering stance. It was expected of a Dothveran Dragon to protect his own Keeper but Reikiila had never seen Dothvera Ferrucio this close up before.

The dragon stood and stared at the man until he cowered and apologised. Dothvera Ferrucio was a wise dragon. He knew that Reikiila had simply stepped too far into his own pride, but Bobby needed to feel safe and strong right now and Dothvera Ferrucio knew that this was something he could do for the boy. After all a Keeper and his Dothveran Dragon were bound to each other to protect each other forever.

Hakramen spoke up next. "C'mon Bobby," she said "Find Pocromethrah. C'mon Bobby."

Dothvera Ferrucio stepped back to allow the boy some space. Bobby closed his eyes to focus and repeated the words of Hakramen in his mind "C'mon Bobby," he said to himself imagining.

When he opened his eyes, the image before him was one of true wonder and amazement. Yes, these Keepers had seen a lot of wonderful things in Shamlu, but to have paper appear from nowhere, land into their hands and open up into Butterflies, who sat still for a moment before taking flight was something else. They still couldn't believe it.

But Reikiila began to laugh at the boy.

As he did, Bobby felt the anger boiling up inside him. He wanted to take revenge on the old man and an image came into his mind that played out before him in a way that he wasn't expecting. The boy watched as the butterfly transformed into a huge angry spider that began to attack Reikiila.

131

Dothvera, noticing this, begged Bobby to change the spider back. Bobby didn't really want to, as he was rather happy at seeing Reikiila so frightened. Suddenly, the spider bit the man and he curled up onto the floor throwing his arm into his side and screaming in pain. It was unlike anything Bobby had ever heard or seen.

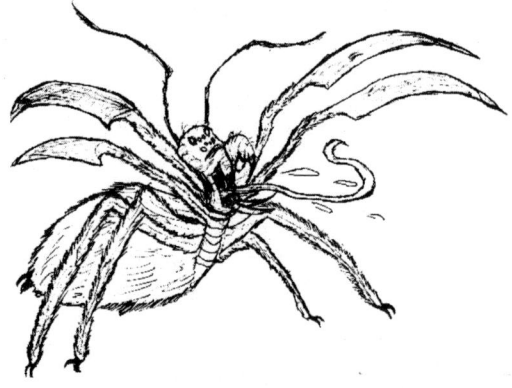

Bobby visualised the spider turning to dust and desperately tried to stop anything else from happening. The spider suddenly stopped attacking and fell into a pile of dust on the ground. Bobby stood watching in panic.

What had he just done?

Dothvera Velara stared at Bobby and hissed at him in anger. Bobby cowered behind Dothvera Ferrucio but he knew that what he had done was not a good thing. As the other Keepers ran to Reikiila's aid, Bobby walked away nervously.

"Pocromethrah?" he heard Hakramen calling. "Pocromethrah?" Bobby's guilt made him return and he ran back to the scene of Reikiila lying on the floor almost cold and his face turning a darker shade of blue, as though he was struggling to breathe.

"Use your magic please?" begged Hakramen.
"What?" asked Bobby.
"Imagine him healed," she said desperately. The Keepers and dragons all turned to the boy in request.

Bobby closed his eyes and imagined Reikiila breathing okay again. He opened his eyes to see if anything was happening.

"It's not working!!" He shouted.
"You have to believe Bobby." answered Dothvera.
"Believe you can do this Bobby!" called out Dothvera again.

Bobby closed his eyes again. He opened them and Reikiila was still on the floor struggling to survive. He decided to keep his eyes closed and clenched his fists and believed as much as he could. Suddenly, things went quiet and peaceful around him. Like a storm had just calmed and all was well again.

"Oh!! You did it!!!" cried out Hakramen and lifted Bobby's arm in the air. "You are indeed Pocromethrah!" called out Hakramen and Totomal walked up to Bobby, "Pocromethrah. Thank you," he said and shook Bobby's hand nodding his head in acceptance. Reikiila, who was still recovering from his ordeal walked over to the boy.

"There is no doubt in my mind Pocromethrah." The man bowed his head to Bobby in agreement with all the other Keepers. This was indeed someone with a powerful mind and a powerful ally to have, but not an enemy to be making.

Things went quiet for a moment with the dragons and the Keepers. Bobby felt awkward too. After all, he had nearly killed someone. He hadn't meant to. He still wasn't quite sure what had happened, but it had. He decided to ask Dothvera what he thought about it all. After all, the dragon was the wisest he had ever known.

"Dothvera?" asked Bobby walking up to the dragon who was sitting down contemplating the world.
"Oh, hello Pocromethrah." the dragon winked at Bobby which made him feel a bit less uncomfortable.

"About earlier..." the boy began but was interrupted by some wise words.

"Ahh yes. Interesting turn of events I would say." smiled Dothvera Ferrucio. After all, what had just happened, as awkward as it may have felt for all involved, had just made each and every Keeper want Bobby or Pocromethrah on their side. Even though that wasn't what the boy had intended.

"But aren't you angry?" asked Bobby.

"You didn't mean to do it, as you said." the dragon replied calmly. "Look Bobby. Shall I still call you Bobby?" the boy nodded. He wasn't used to his new name yet.

"The thing that you must remember Bobby is that everyone realises that you did not mean to seriously hurt anyone, or you wouldn't have tried to save him and you wouldn't have succeeded. The thing I think is amazing is that you didn't believe you were that powerful and now, through this series of events which has maybe taught someone a lesson but not actually hurt anyone seriously, you have shown everyone and yourself that you are capable of anything you desire. You also have the compassion to save someone whom you are not sure would ever have saved you. I, for one, think that is something to be proud of."

"But how did it hurt him so badly Dothvera. I only wanted to scare him a little. I didn't imagine it doing that."

"You just need to tweak your thoughts a little more. You're not practiced enough."

Practice. It was a word that Bobby would be hearing a lot from now on. It was important that he knew how to use his mind for the good and how to control it so that things didn't get out of hand. He understood now, that practice was really important and that maybe he shouldn't have been so upset about it in the first place. Bobby now knew that practice was the best thing to do.

Dothvera Ferrucio looked down to Bobby and saw that he was watching the other Keepers who were all sitting on a pile of rocks nearby and seemed a little bit quiet. The dragon nudged the boy towards them with the edge of his tail. Bobby felt himself being pushed closer to where the Keepers were.

"Go on." whispered the dragon to Bobby in his mind.

Bobby walked over to Hakramen who was sitting down not far from him.

"Hey," said Bobby nervously.
"Hey." answered Hakramen.

"Are you okay?" the boy asked. He was not quite sure what to say.

"Yep." Hakramen answered quietly.

"I didn't mean to..."

"I know." she interrupted. "It's just taken us a bit by surprise that's all." Hakramen looked over to Reikiila who was still recovering from the spider incident.

"You know," continued Hakramen, "He's not all that bad. He did save me once. He just doubts things. Well, he doubts people mainly and sometimes he's been right." Bobby looked over to Reikiila. Suddenly the man didn't seem all that threatening at all. In fact, he seemed rather vulnerable.

"Why don't you go and say hello, eh?" Hakramen said encouragingly. Bobby was nervous, but he agreed that he should probably try to speak to Reikiila. After all, he did owe him an explanation at least. He had hurt the man badly. Not intentionally of course. Now Bobby hoped that what Dothvera had said was right. He hoped that everyone did realise he hadn't meant it. Either way, this was his chance to regain everyone's trust. Bobby walked over to Reikiila.

"Hi,"

"Hi." answered Reikiila.

"You know I didn't mean for it to go that far, yes?"

"I know," said Reikiila, seeming a little more nervous now.

Bobby realised that it was time to break the ice properly, so he pushed the conversation a little further.

"So, why are you intense and wise? How did you get your name?" Reikiila looked up to the boy who was standing in front of him.

"I am intense because when I fight anything, I am 100% focussed and I am wise because I have a lot of life experience. Especially here in Shamlu." answered Reikiila.

"I think that you must be a great warrior." said Bobby.

"I have fought before and I will always be there for Shamlu."

Bobby smiled.

"I am sorry I hurt you," he said and turned to walk away.

"Pocromethrah?" Reikiila said and Bobby turned his head around to look Reikiila in the eye. "I am sorry I taunted you." Reikiila gave Bobby a knowing smile and Bobby walked away knowing that he and the old man had finally seen eye to eye. They were going to be fine from now on. Maybe Dothvera had been right.

Totomal was the last person that Bobby wanted to talk to. He stood up when Bobby arrived and shook his hand. Totomal had been quite quiet since Bobby had shown his true powers and Bobby had noticed this. The boy wished to put things right, but he wasn't sure how.

Totomal, who was known for his speed in the battle training grounds was generally a quiet man, but he respected this young boy for what he had done earlier that day. Totomal hadn't been a Keeper for as long as the others and he was still learning. He had been in training for a long time but had never had to banish a dark creature to Dahkrath nor had he fought one as Hakramen and Reikiila had. These days it was rare to see a monster of Dahkrath however, things changed often in Shamlu and sometimes the keepers had to face scary things and find a way to protect the good in this world. Totomal and Bobby smiled at each other.

"I am glad that you are Pocromethrah. We need you to be that. It was the missing piece in this team of Keepers." said Totomal.

"Thank you." responded Bobby realising that although Totomal had little to say. When he did speak his words were always the wisest.

"I look forward to seeing what other surprises you have for us." said Totomal with a nod and a wink.

"Pocromethrah." said Dothvera Cherama, interrupting the conversation. "We need to speak to you." Bobby nodded and headed over to the dragon, who wrapped his tail around the boy's waist and gently lifted him onto his back. Totomal watched as Bobby took to the sky and all three dragons followed Dothvera Cherama and headed into the distance before they disappeared behind the clouds.

"Am I in trouble?" asked Bobby as he was placed on the floor in between all four dragons. They were around him in a circle and began to lower their heads to look closer at him.

"You made us realise the wonders of your power Pocromethrah and we are not angry. We are amazed at what you are capable of, but we must ask you to train harder from now on as this power of yours is not something to be played with. It is equal to playing with fire. Do you understand? You must learn to respect your gift."

Bobby still wasn't used to being called Pocromethrah. It was a long name, but he understood why he was given that name. He wasn't aware of how powerful he was in Shamlu and it had scared him a little more since he had lost his temper with Reikiila.

"The extra training will begin immediately. With each of us you must learn to connect and create and protect. Do you have any questions?" Dothvera Cherama asked the boy.

There was only one question that Bobby could think of asking this huge and wonderful dragon, but it scared him to ask. He wasn't sure if the answer would be one that he wanted to hear. However, this was the best time to ask. Now that all the dragons were present.

"If I do this for you then all I ask is that you promise me on the life of all that remain in Shamlu, that you will take me home once you are done with me and that I am back in time for tea with my mum in my world. Can you promise this?"

The dragons were a little taken aback with how confidently Bobby was speaking to them about this, but also, they understood that the boy was homesick and wanted to see his family again. They knew that Robert J Bobcat had often felt the same.

They whispered amongst themselves in Shamlen and Bobby could not pick out any words that they were saying. Finally, they all looked down to

Bobby and said one word, "Amentha." then Dothvera Ferrucio translated. "It is done Bobby. The dragons have agreed that they will make sure you are home for tea, but now we must move quickly. The intensive training must begin. Come with us,"

CHAPTER 11

Practicing power

Bobby followed the dragons to a space where they could train together.

Whispering amongst themselves in Shamlen, they then translated to Bobby what was going to happen next.

"Pocromethrah. We would like you to learn the skills of Acmemento your ancestor and begin mastering your mind. She had many skills such as translating Shamlen, imagining defence weaponry on the spot, transporting herself from one dragon to another with immediate effect and many more.

"Her transfer time from imagining a thing into existence and it being in existence was half a millisecond. She was the fastest mind creator that has ever been and will ever be again and now it is time that you begin walking in her footsteps. Firstly, we will begin with translating Shamlen directly into your first language."

The dragons leaned in towards Bobby and Dothvera Ferrucio continued to speak.

"Imagine that as the words are leaving our minds, they are transforming and twisting and turning and forcing themselves into your language before they get to your mind Bobby." Bobby frowned for a moment, not quite sure what Dothvera Ferrucio had meant.

"What do you mean?" he asked.
"Picture them Bobby. Try now, close your eyes."
Bobby closed his eyes.

"Now imagine, Pocromethrah. Imagine that every time I speak, as if by some kind of magic the words floated through air and slowed down their sound and before they became words in your ear; they transformed and translated themselves into a language you could hear and understand." Bobby squeezed his eyes shut and tried to do what Dothvera Ferrucio had told him.

The dragons began to speak in their own language in full sentences, but he still couldn't work out how to understand what they were saying. He opened his eyes and the dragons stopped.

"It's not working."

Dothvera Velara huffed loudly and spoke to Dothvera Ferrucio in Shamlen. Bobby suddenly wished he could hear what the dragons were muttering about above his head, but no matter how hard he tried, he could only get bits of half words coming through. For example: When Dothvera Velara said that the boy had no sense because he did not realise what the word practice meant.

All Bobby had heard was "e as o nse" instead of "He has no sense." When he told Dothvera what was happening, the dragon couldn't believe how quickly he had begun to receive pieces of translation, even if they were only small pieces at a time.

"I tell you what. Just imagine full words Pocromethrah, instead of bits of words. Try to imagine the full sentences getting through to you. You're getting there. It takes time you know. This takes incredible skill."

Bobby closed his eyes. The dragon interrupted him.

"Bobby try to do this without closing your eyes. Try to do this with your eyes open. Closing your eyes doesn't make your power stronger, okay?" the boy nodded. He almost went to close his eyes again, but then remembering what he had just been told, he opened his eyes and saw the dragons readying themselves for conversation.

He could see Dothvera Potentioh, the sunset-coloured dragon begin to speak. He stopped himself from thinking that the Shamlen language was going to come out in the sound of the dragons voice and he pictured the words coming out of the dragons mouth and translating themselves in front of him. Then he imagined hearing something he could understand. Dothvera Potentioh said something simple enough for Bobby to translate and repeated the same sentence over and over. The dragon guessed this might work.

At first Bobby heard a jumble of letters, "m ago at eats r?" his mind asked, what could that be? Then he began to see Dothvera Potentioh speak again. "I e drag at eats ar" Bobby heard and wondered what exactly "I e drag at eats ar" meant.

Dothvera Potentioh kept repeating.

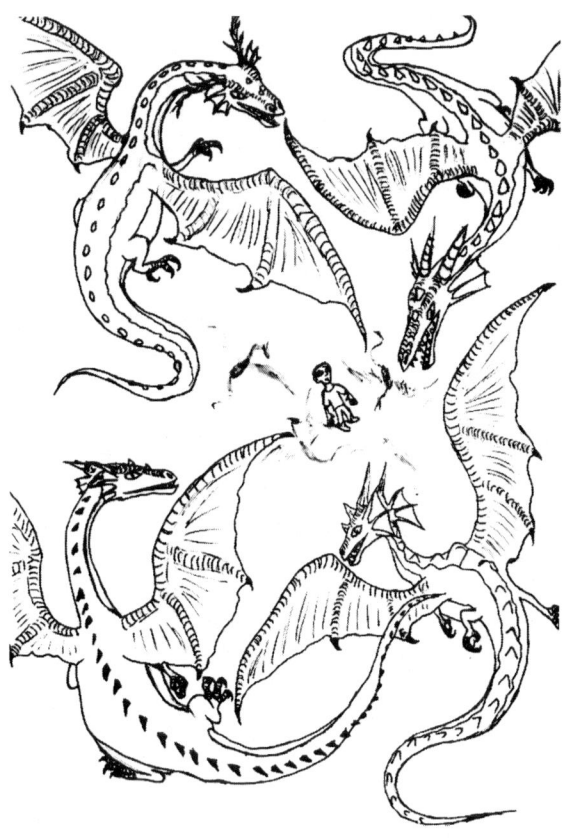

"I te agon ta eats ir" Bobby listened harder and imagined deeper.

"I the agon hat eats air" Bobby listened more. "I'm the ragon hat eats air" he heard. But the sentence still wasn't making sense. Bobby tried even harder to hear what the dragon had to say.

147

"I am e ragon tat eats air," Bobby suddenly shouted.

"I am the dragon that eats air!" he cried excitedly.

The doorway dragons began to laugh and laugh and laugh. If you've ever been in the presence of a dragon that laughs or coughs, you would realise that for little boys like Bobby it is quite scary.

All of a sudden he heard all the dragons and saw them spitting out different things. Dothvera Potentioh threw everything around him into chaos as huge wafts of rushing air came out from his mouth. Dothvera Velara showered Bobby with water. From Dothvera Cherama bits of rock and mud spat in all directions and of course Dothvera Ferrucio laughed out smoke and sparks of fire.

Bobby dodged as big blobs of water, earth and charred air nearly landed on him.

"Oh wait!" thought Bobby suddenly realising what had made all the dragons laugh so much. "I know it!" shouted Bobby.

"I am the dragon that BREATHES air!!!!"

"Indeed!" answered Dothvera Ferrucio. "But Bobby, you must learn to translate quickly. You cannot be guessing. If something serious

148

happens you might need to hear what we say immediately, as quickly as you hear me now. Speaking in your language. We will keep practicing."

The dragons seemed to like practicing, but Bobby sometimes found it difficult to keep up with the pace. It was like revising a million subjects all at once and it was extremely tiring.

"Okay, let's try again." said Dothvera Ferrucio for the gazillienth time. But Bobby was losing patience.

"NO!" he replied, taking the dragons by surprise. "But Bobby, we need to train you," said the dragon.
"I don't want to," answered the boy desperately.

Dothvera Ferrucio realised that training was going to be difficult for Bobby. He wasn't used to staying focused. But in order to get him up to the standard he needed to be, he needed to train and train hard. Realising that Bobby might be bored of trying to translate Shamlen, Dothvera Ferrucio tried something else. Something he wasn't sure if Bobby was ready for, but that he had to try and find out. He left Bobby for a moment to give him a break while he spoke to the other dragons.

Bobby tried to make out what they were saying but could only pick up patches of words here and there.

The dragons came back to Bobby and asked him if he could try something with them. They wanted to find out if he could create his own defence mechanisms in the face of fear.

"Now Pocromethrah, if you can do this it is the greatest test of faith in oneself that I could ever ask of you. Will you trust us and try this?" Bobby not realising quite what he was agreeing to, nodded and agreed without a second thought. However, upon facing this fear, he had wished he hadn't agreed to the dragons request so easily. For as the boy stood where he was told to, Dothvera Velara landed directly ahead of him and proceeded to breathe in and without any warning Bobby saw a large rush of water, that looked like the size of a huge lake heading towards him in one straight line.

Dothvera Ferrucio called out to Bobby to protect himself but Bobby froze still. He watched as the water got closer and closer and at the last minute, he put up his arms to cover his eyes. Suddenly, Bobby realised that he was unscathed. He opened his eyes to see what he had done, but he hadn't done a thing. The water was still directly in front of him, so close he could almost touch it, it had changed direction and was heading to the left of

Bobby in a long line, as far as the eye could see. To the right, Bobby could see Dothvera Potentioh breathing out a huge gust of air that had redirected the water away from him.

The sounds around Bobby were like that of a thunderstorm. He could hear the patter of water like raindrops that were spraying out from the huge wall of redirected water and he could hear the gust of air blowing from the right of him. Dothvera Velara closed his mouth and soon the water began to stop.

Bobby's face was white with fear.

"It's okay Bobby. Maybe another time, hmm?" said Dothvera Ferrucio and the dragons nodded amongst themselves as the dragon told his brothers he was taking the boy to have a sleep.

Bobby woke up back in the towers on his unicorn feather bed.

"I'm sorry," he said to Dothvera Ferrucio who was sitting watching over him.
"For what Pocromethrah?" the dragon enquired.
"Don't call me that." Bobby replied. "Pocromethrah would have been able to build a wall between him and that water. I failed. I am just Bobby." The dragon sighed a deep and thoughtful sigh.

"Hmmm," he said, "You know Pocromethrah is Bobby, don't you? He is just Bobby in this world. In your world, you are still Bobby. Bobby Bobcat will always be a magnificent name to have in both this world and the others."

"Others?" asked Bobby curiously.

"Let me continue a moment." said the wise dragon. "You see Bobby. You are Pocromethrah. You were when you entered this world through a magical force. You were someone that we could only refer to as a powerful mind. Your mind is powerful already."

"But...."

"But the thing you must remember is that even a powerful mind must be taught. There is no easy fix for training yourself at your skills. You must and you will train yourself daily and practice until you are in control of this powerful mind of yours. That was a test. An exam of some sort. Now we know the extent of your skills, we know where to focus our next lessons. Do you see Bobby? And failure is not failure. It is simply learning. No one gets it right all the time. We all learn from our mistakes. Without failure, success would not exist."

Bobby went quiet. He had learned a lot recently and the lessons just seemed to keep coming. He knew he had to get used to learning and training and practicing.

"You will always be a work in progress Bobby. Even as Pocromethrah. Everyone is."

Bobby nodded.

"Dothvera?" he asked
"Yes."
"Why are you training me so much? Why do YOU need ME? I'm just a boy. You're a dragon. Dragons are wonderful and strong and powerful creatures, and you are wise. How can I be so important?" Dothvera Ferrucio smiled at the young boy's innocence.

"I don't think you realise Bobby. You are stronger and certainly more powerful than me or any of my brothers. Here in Shamlu, you are the greatest power there is. I keep trying to remind you of this, but I think you are still thinking that this is like your world. This is nothing like your world Bobby. In your world, power like yours is often taken for granted. In your world, though you might have strength of character, it is not accepted as a power. In your world physical strength is applauded more than mental strength. Here Bobby, you rule over everything and we know it. Your strength of mind is recognised as a skill here in Shamlu. Your great grandmother, your grandfather and many before you have known the power that you hold right there in your own head. It is the power of imagination and little does your world know, but it is the greatest power of all. With it, you can create anything you could ever wish for."

Anything he could ever wish for? Bobby started to wonder something. Something he had not considered before now. If the dragons believed he could create anything he could wish for. Why couldn't he wish himself back home. Why couldn't he imagine his way out of this world?

Little did Bobby know, but the Dothveran dragons were listening in on his thoughts and they were glad to hear what Bobby was thinking about. Finally, the penny had dropped. Finally, Pocromethrah was beginning to take things into his own hands. Finally, Bobby was becoming the Pocromethrah they had always hoped he would be.

CHAPTER 12

The secret plan

Bobby knew he couldn't tell anyone about his plans to get back home. He knew that if he thought about it too much when the dragons were too close, they may even find out. He didn't want the dragons to know that he was planning an escape from Shamlu. He did not realise that they already knew his thinking and were already listening to his every thought. So, he had started to work on a secret plan.

Little did Bobby know, but ever since he had begun to transfer thoughts to the Dothveran dragons, they had been able to listen to everything he was thinking. They didn't want to tell him this of course. Dragons were very mystical creatures with many powers.

They were the kind of creatures that had existed in so many imaginary ways, so many times that they had developed all the powers of all the dragons that had ever been imagined in the manlands. The Dothveran dragons even had powers and magic that they did not even know of. Without Bobby realising, he was transferring every thought he had at every moment to the dragons and they were listening in. This meant that they had to be wise or they could unintentionally disrupt destiny.

The dragons left Bobby alone for a while to talk amongst themselves while he started thinking about what it was that he needed for his escape. First, he needed a pen and some paper, so he tried to use his power to bring them about. He imagined himself sitting with a pen and paper in his hand and closed his eyes tightly because he found it easier to imagine this way.

He saw himself writing a plan out on some paper in the room he was in. He opened his eyes and saw that a pen and paper had appeared in the room. Then he noticed that another pen and paper had appeared. Then another began to appear so he tried to close his eyes and picture just one. He only needed one pen and paper to be left behind for him. When he had accomplished this, he picked up the pen and paper and began to write.

'My secret plan – part one'
"Hmm." thought Bobby "What can I do?"

While Bobby was working out his plan, the dragon brothers gathered to talk about what Bobby was doing.

"Vere mucho alles do arela mere ucho." ("we must leave him alone more often.") said Dothvera Cherama

"oot, womah de alleser a octiay reprisee?" ("But what if he leaves and never returns?") asked Dothvera Ferrucio who had grown rather fond of his young friend.

"Seh de nahyeh reprisee, dos nah cra oin vere toolu de itt." ("If he does not return, he is not the one we think he is.")

As he said these words each of his brothers looked at Dothvera Cherama with fear in their eyes and began to mutter in panic.

"Oot seh dos nah Pocromethrah, womah huveh? Iv ittera lotra. Darmapetth itterah hera!" ("But if he's not Pocromethrah, what happens? It will be too late. Darmapetth will be here!")

"De mucho cra oin!" ("He must be the one!")

"Dos cra oin." ("He is the one.")

"Yeeyo ov hoz de arrieh hera!" ("Look at how he came here!")

"Oot, womah seh dos nah?" ("But what if he isn't?")

The words of panic from the dragons were getting louder by the minute. Dothvera Cherama couldn't have this. What if the boy heard the words the dragons were saying?

Suddenly the large dragon stood up and shouted as loud as his voice could carry. "NAHMHOYA!!" (STOP!!") he shouted. Sitting thousands of miles away in the towers, Bobby heard the dragons voice loud and clear.

"Nahmhoya." Said Dothvera Cherama, "Vere nah mucho wratha. Vere nah mucho awayu destruccio omohcru ve. Seh dos nah Pocromethrah, ella anmerah ittera graspeh do ploteh. Vere ittera vitweh Darmapetth. Ivoh nah ittera reduccio ac wou vollos hera."

("We must not argue. We must not let fear overcome us. If he is not Pocromethrah then another will take his place. We will survive Darmapetth. There will be no end to our worlds here.")

The dragons looked at their brother and tried to believe that they would all survive what was foretold to be the end of their world: Darmapetth.

It was prophesised that on the 20th Night of Darkness, there was to be a force of evil that would threaten Shamlu and everything around it.

On Dothvera Ferrucio's travels with Sir Robert J Bobcat, they had met a see-er who had foretold such things. The see-er had also spoken of a boy. Seemingly too young, but exceptionally skilled at Imaginerah, the powers of imagining things into being.

Sir Robert J Bobcat never knew that one day his grandson would get carried away into Shamlu without a key. Could this little boy sitting in the dragon's home thousands of skies away be the person who could save them and all they had ever known? They hoped so.

Back at Dothvera Ferrucio's towering home in the clouds of Shamlu, Bobby was finally coming up with some ideas for a plan. He would have to learn how to think up a way out that only he could use from Shamlu. Possibly a separate doorway to his own world. But where could he possibly find that?

The dragons were the doorways, but he had seen other creatures in Shamlu. But how could he convince a unicorn to fly him home and even if he could, how would he know the way? A million questions flew into Bobby's mind all at once. Was he really going to be able to do this all by himself?

The Dothveran dragons had continued their conversation about Bobby, and they had all come to an agreement that they would trust him to leave and hope he would come back to Shamlu. Dothvera Ferrucio was to continue teaching the boy as much as possible. The daily intensive training would also continue, but Bobby was to be given more freedom. Freedom to wander the hallways of the towers and he was to be allowed time to spend with the other Keepers. The dragons had also decided to see if the Keepers would come to trust Bobby enough to help him. They wanted to see what would happen if Bobby asked them for help.

This was the greatest test of all. Would Bobby find a way home? Would he bring a trusted keeper to help him? Would he get home? And if he did would he ever come back to Shamlu again?

Pocromethrah would.
But would Bobby Bobcat?

Only time would tell.

"You've been a long time Dothvera. I almost fell asleep." said Bobby on the dragons return to the five towers.

"My brothers and I were working out what your next training must be. It took some time. Some of us thought it should be harder and that you should have no free time at all..."

Bobby's eyes opened wide with fear at the thought of being in constant and relentless training with the dragons.

"But others of us..." Dothvera Ferrucio continued, "...thought you should have some time to gather your thoughts in between and study in your own time too."

The dragon stopped for a breath. But Bobby was eager to know what he and his brothers had decided.

"So, what happened??!!" Bobby asked.
"Hmm?"
"What did you decide?"

"Oh, I see. We decided that everyone was right, so we have split your days into parts of very intensive training and very relaxed training so that you have the benefit of both."
"YES!" thought Bobby.

And Dothvera Ferrucio heard it loud and clear.

Bobby woke up and realised that it was time to begin his new day of training. It was weird not having night-time. Bobby remembered how he used to look out of his bedroom window with amazement at the brightness of the moon against the darkness of the night sky, often lit up with stars that twinkled. He did miss night skies. He wondered why there were no night skies in Shamlu. It did seem very odd for it to always be daytime.

"Time to get up!" roared Dothvera Ferrucio overhead. "Can't sleep forever my boy, this is your training time."

After hours and hours spent in training with the dragons and trying to learn how to create a magical shield for himself, Bobby headed back to the towers to do his own studying for the first time. He came back from his training with a cardboard shield, a magical fluffy shield and a shield made of buttons. It wasn't always easy to conjure up exactly what he wanted in record time with a bunch of dragons watching over him. But Bobby was glad that training hadn't lasted so long this time, and that he could begin working on his new plan.

After training, Dothvera Ferrucio took Bobby into a room that was the largest of its kind. It connected to the meeting room in the centre tower and was an amazing sight to see. It was the dragon's library. The books in this library were the largest books Bobby had ever seen.

Bobby looked around in amazement, at the room that went higher than he could see and stretched out further than he could tell. In the one corner was a section that looked just about right for Bobby. It was full of human sized books.

Gesturing to the smallest section of the library, Dothvera said, "This is where we kept the books your grandfather brought here from the manlands. All about the history of earth and how it has evolved over time. He would often bring books back here to show me," smiled Dothvera Ferrucio thinking fondly of his old friend.

Bobby looked up at the dragon, "Am I anything like my grandfather?" he asked. Dothvera smiled.

"Oh, he was adventurous and clever and a great imaginer. Not the best, but he practiced every day and there were many things he managed to do. I was glad of this as he always wanted to be better at it, but imagination is a skill. Not everyone can do it well, because you have to forget about reality and that can be difficult. Not everyone is a natural like you Bobby. You have to go deep into your own mind and focus all your attention on imagining, and that's what people find so difficult especially as they grow up."

The boy's face lit up whilst listening to stories of his grandfather. Grandpa Bobcat had always told his grandson stories about the amazing adventures he had been on. His mother often said that he shouldn't tell Bobby so many stories, in case Bobby believed what the old man said. But now Bobby knew why the adventures sounded so real and why his grandfather was so good at coming up with so many. It was because the stories Grandpa Bobcat were telling his grandson were 100% true!

Bobby couldn't take his eyes off the sheer quantity of books in this room, let alone the shelves upon shelves of books in the corner that his grandfather had created. This room was spectacular!

"Here, take this one first..." Dothvera Ferrucio said, nudging out a book that looked remarkably similar to one of the books he had been sitting on when Bobby had first met him on the windowsill.

"Your grandfather transcribed the whole book from your grandmother's. No other group of Keepers have been allowed in this library because this contains all the information they would ever need to know, and this library is protected by magic. Only those of a noble heart and spirit can enter. I knew you would be fine Bobby." Bobby wondered.

"But what if I wasn't pure of heart?" the boy asked.
"Oh, never you mind." answered the dragon.

It was a good job Bobby didn't know the danger of entering the dragon's library if you weren't pure of heart and spirit. But Dothvera Ferrucio knew in his dragon heart that Bobby would walk through without harm, because dragons can see hearts and can see the purity of them.

"Time to study now Pocromethrah," said the dragon. Without saying another word, he left Bobby sitting alone at a small table in the human sized section of the library.

"But?" asked Bobby, however the dragon had gone.

Bobby sat in the large room feeling rather lonely. He decided that the best thing to do before he scared himself and allowed Boglets to get to him, was to read a book and forget about how quiet and eerie this room was without anyone to fill it.

He picked up the book, opened the pages and began to read his grandmother's journal from the beginning this time.

This book is a book all about the wonders of Shamlu. A world that I have discovered and written about so that I can remember everything I have learned. Shamlu is a most wondrous place full of incredible and amazing creatures of all kinds. It has actual flying and fire breathing dragons and it is full of creatures I have tried to give names to, that represent them as best as I can. I have filled this book with all that I know and have learned and continue to learn. Please keep it safe as there are secrets in this book that could expose Shamlu and all of its wonders to a world that I do not think could ever understand it or keep it safe, my world.

Love and best wishes to you,
Amelia Bobcat

It still thrilled Bobby to be reading his own great grandmother's journal and to think that she was the one who had discovered this amazing world. She must have been an incredible woman.

Bobby remembered when Dothvera Ferrucio had gone through this book the first time, but he couldn't remember everything, because he didn't understand much of it then. Now it was different. He understood a whole lot more this time. The map of Shamlu was on the next page and it seemed to make more sense now. As Bobby scanned over the map, he noticed something unique. Shamlu connected to something. A word that Bobby couldn't quite understand. The word 'Elsanthah' was written on the edge of Shamlu, which was then connected to another place called 'Remero'. Both these words confused Bobby. He tried to imagine himself seeing the right word on the page, but when he opened his eyes, the letters had just mixed up and confused him even more. He tried to remember the two words. Elsan... something and Remero.

Bobby studied the image a little bit more and noticed that there was a note added to the bottom of the page. It looked like someone else had written something in small handwriting

"yeeyo hera, meerah itt eena molebrocha boveh"

He needed to practice translating Shamlen a whole lot more for this to work. He took out his little notebook and pen, which he had hidden in his trouser pocket and began to write:

"MUST LEARN TO TRANSLATE SHAMLEN, GO BACK TO PG 4 OF AMELIA'S JOURNAL WHEN READY!"

Just then as he was putting his notebook away, Hakramen appeared.

"Hey Pocromethrah!" she said happily, "Studying?"
"Yes." answered Bobby quickly, aware that he'd just been caught putting his secret notebook away.

"I remember studying in here with your very own Sir Robert J Bobcat, or as we knew him Granfairdd ov Dothvera. He was a great teacher, very patient and wise. Like a grandfather would be I suppose. Did you know him well?" Hakramen asked, sitting at the small wooden desk that Bobby was reading Amelia's journal on.

"He was like a father to me." answered Bobby, who had wished he had got to know his grandfather better before he had passed away. Bobby lowered his head thinking about the moment his grandfather had left. Hakramen held his chin and lifted it up.

"You know Bobby, he and you are very much alike. He was wise, but fearless too. He was an adventurer and he had a great imagination. Sometimes he could even imagine things happening and they would come to life like they do for you. He and you will always be connected. He was your grandfather. How amazing is that? Little pieces of him went into creating little pieces of you. He's still here. I see him in your smile and in your spirit. He's still here in Pocromethrah. In you." Bobby's eyes lifted towards Hakramen's. His spirit lifted to think that he reminded her of his grandfather.

Sir Robert J Bobcat had wanted to teach Bobby more about Shamlu after his own son had passed away, but he knew it wasn't his place to teach Bobby back in his own world. He had chosen to respect his mother's wishes. Although Daniel Bobcat was meant to have trained his son in certain aspects of the Shamlen language and in the ways of the magical world, he had died before he had had the chance to. So Bobby was left to discover his destiny on his own.

Maybe that's what had made the boy so important. Maybe he was young enough to do this because he still had his wonderful imagination fully intact. Maybe that was why everything had happened the way it had. Only destiny knew the true answers to these questions. Life always has a way of bringing us through the journeys we need the most. Even though Bobby didn't realise it, he would soon begin to learn that everything he had been through was for a reason.

"Your grandfather was the greatest explorer that there ever was." continued Hakramen. "He kept a journal. It should be in here somewhere. I don't know where it ended up, but he did say he would leave it in a safe place and hand it to someone very important. I imagine that was Dothvera Cherama." As Hakramen uttered those words, the very dragon she was speaking of landed in the room seemingly from above and spoke quickly.

"Pocromethrah. Training begins."
The dragon picked the boy up out of his seat with his tail and within seconds Bobby was riding out of the Dragon's Library.

Bobby and Dothvera Cherama landed in a place that seemed deserted but that was also very beautiful. For miles around there were beautiful fields of green grass that stretched as far as the eye could see. Bobby had seen fields before, but not like this. These fields linked onto other fields that were surrounded by the largest of mountains.

This stretch of land looked like it was large enough to contain many dragons.

Dothvera told Bobby what was going to happen next.

"We are going to shout words to you Pocromethrah and your job is to try to decipher the words we are saying. One of us will call out in Shamlen and you must focus enough to hear the word. Then you must write it down."

Bobby was all of a sudden concerned that the dragons had known his secret, he almost gave his game away by touching his pocket to get his notebook, but before he did that Dothvera Cherama pointed to a space beside him where a quill and paper were already laid out.

Bobby sighed a huge sigh of relief as he picked up the quill and paper. Little did he know that every dragon there knew exactly what he was sighing about.

At the beginning Bobby was struggling to get the full words translated, but because he knew this skill was going to help him decipher Amelia's journal and the words written in it, he worked much harder to focus his mind. This time he listened more to the advice that the Dothveran Dragons were giving to him.

"Concentrate Pocromethrah!"

"Listen inside,"

"Try not to think too much!"

"Just keep practicing, it will get easier!"

Bobby took some deep breaths in and focused as much as he could. This was going to take some real effort on his part. He focused and then breathed out and suddenly, he heard it.

"Mewehmah!" ("Mountain!") called Dothvera Cherama.

"Emwayah!" ("Unicorn!") called another.

"Voufer!" ("Wings!") called Dothvera Ferrucio.

The dragons watched and noticed. Down below them, the boy began to write down the exact words they were saying in English.

"Perfect!" called out Dothvera Cherama. Whether or not he was speaking in Shamlen, Bobby couldn't tell as each word he heard was in perfect English.

"By the way, I am speaking in Shamlen!" winked the dragon. Bobby smiled a deep smile. Now he could translate every word the dragons said. Eager to get back to the book to translate that too. Bobby asked Dothvera Ferrucio to take him back to the Dragon's Library.

"Tomorrow." answered the dragon.

High up in the skies, the dragons met to talk about Bobby as he slept a little.

"I don't like it!" said Dothvera Ferrucio.
"We're teaching him to betray us." he continued.

"Give it time Ferrucio. He is putting more effort into his practices and that is a good thing. Let go of him a little and if he comes back, he will be stronger." The dragons whispered so as not to wake the boy, as dragons speaking are very loud. They are as loud as two clouds crashing together in the skies and can easily be heard by humans below.

Bobby, who still couldn't sleep, sat below the dragons listening to the whispering but not able to make out a single word, because they were so far up into the skies and so quiet it was hard to hear and understand them.

The boy was excited about tomorrow. He decided that rather than say anything in case of the dragons heard it, he would write in his notebook. "Tomorrow I will translate the map," he wrote. The dragons heard him as he scribbled the words onto the page.

"TOMORROW I WILL DECIPHER THE MAP!"

CHAPTER 13

The perfectly sized plane

Bobby couldn't wait to get himself to the Dragon's Library and find out what the map was trying to tell him in Shamlen. He woke up eager to get started. Dothvera was already waiting for him when he awoke.

"More studying this morning Bobby!" said Dothvera Ferrucio, before leading him through the tower's large hallways to the wonderful Dragon's library. Bobby had to admit that he did love the look of this place. It was so big that even he couldn't tell where it began and where it ended, but there was also something so magical and mysterious about it. It was quite an amazing place to be. Bobby had been on many school visits to many libraries before, but they had not quite impressed him like this one.

Dothvera Ferrucio was curious about Bobby and he wanted to be able to trust the boy, so he decided to ask him what he would be studying today to see what he would say.

"I'm still trying to read Amelia's Journal," answered Bobby being as honest as he could be to the dragon. Dothvera smiled. At least by reading what the boy was thinking he now knew that he didn't want to hide anything from him. He was just trying to get home because he loved his mum. That was different. Dothvera Ferrucio was the sentimental type and he understood that Bobby had a dream to get home first. He was also fairly sure that if he ever did get home, he would find his way back to Shamlu.

Bobby looked at the desk and the book that was already open on the page he had been studying. Dothvera Cherama had quickly escorted him away so the book was just as Bobby had left it.

He quickly scanned the page, but he still saw the Shamlen words that he had seen before. He looked up at Dothvera Ferrucio.

"Everything okay lad?" asked the dragon.
"Yes." answered Bobby not wanting to give anything away.

Dothvera Ferrucio felt Bobby's awkwardness and smiled again, seeing that the boy had a conscience after all.

When the dragon left, Bobby put his head in his hands and sighed deeply. "No, no, no," he said to himself. "How can I find a way to translate writing?"

"Maybe there's a book on that." answered Hakramen who had just walked into the library to meet Bobby.

"A book! Of course!" said Bobby. "Thanks!" and he quickly began to look through the books on the shelf near him to find a book that might help. Hakramen joined him.

"How do you know when I'm here?" Bobby asked.
"The dragons asked me to help you with your studying. It's nice to know I'm pure of heart, eh?"

"Oh?" said Bobby, "Do they ask you about me?" he asked while they both continued to scan the human sized library.

"Not really. They just said if you need anything to help you to get it, because I've studied in here before,"
"Oh, I see," said Bobby, relieved that the dragons weren't on to him.

176

After scanning the final shelf of books Bobby once again looked distraught.

"Bobby?" asked Hakramen showing her concern "I mean, Pocromethrah of course."
"It's okay to call me what you like," said Bobby
"Well, okay then Bobby. So, what's the matter?"
"I need that book."

The two of them sat at the desk in the human library not quite sure what to do next.

"Wait!" cried Hakramen. "What about the other books?" she said. The two keepers looked out at the Dragons Library in complete wonder. How could they possibly get into those books? They were huge.

"That's impossible." said Bobby.
"Not with you it isn't," said Hakramen smiling.
"What? I can't get up there!"
"But you might be able to imagine a way, hmm? Pocromethrah?"

Bobby thought for a second. Maybe Hakramen was right. Maybe he could imagine a way up there. But even when he was up there how could he get into the books?

"I've seen you do some things I would have called impossible. You are a powerful mind, as we keep telling you and the dragons keep telling you. I think you should learn how to use it to your advantage," said Hakramen smiling.

Bobby sat down and flicked through Amelia's journal and looked up the page he remembered Dothvera Ferrucio reading to him. How to make things happen.

"This is the page!" said Bobby. He scanned through the journal page and said out loud the most important bits.

"Focus!" he read, "Let go of distracting thoughts." he continued to scan, "Believe in your ability." he read the warning at the bottom, "Don't let fear stop your belief!"

"Okay." said Bobby rubbing his hands together. Hakramen watched eagerly, seeing a skilled imaginer at work was a privilege and she knew it.

"I can do this!" said Bobby to himself.

"You CAN!" called out Hakramen.

"Okay imagine." Bobby took a deep breath in, "Wait a minute," he said confused. "What am I meant to be imagining?"

Hakramen stood and thought for a moment and then answered. "Some kind of flying object large enough for us two," she said smiling with excitement at the thought of it.

Bobby prepared himself in his mind. He imagined the picture of him and Hakramen flying off up to a book and he saw them face to face with the book they were looking for. Then he readied his gaze into the space in front of him and waited for the thing to appear. Muttering the words over and over from Amelia's journal, "Believe, focus, let go. Believe, focus, let go."

Incredibly, like a string of magic painting in the air an item of some kind was being drawn into reality.

"Yes!" shouted Hakramen, "You're doing it!"

Bobby focused even more. "Believe, focus, let go." he repeated. "Believe, focus, let go." The magic continued. Hakramen watched in amazement as the image drew itself into the space before their very eyes.

"Believe, focus, let go." Bobby sighed deeply and finally the invisible magic pen stopped.

In front of Bobby and Hakramen was an actual plane. Golden and beautiful but quite small. "It's a bit small," said Hakramen, looking inside of the plane.

"Wow!" she exclaimed. "It has levers and everything. This is a REAL plane!"

Bobby followed Hakramen and looked inside the plane too. It was a real plane.

"What do we do now?" Bobby asked.
"Make it big!" said Hakramen as if it was a 'piece of cake' to do something like that.
"Make it big?" thought Bobby to himself. How could he do that?

"How?" he asked.
"Visualise it!" Hakramen answered. Her eyes beaming with excitement.

"Right!" said Bobby, staring at the small plane in front of him. He thought about it for a second and then began picturing all the sides of the plane expanding and growing and forming into a bigger version. He kept thinking of it and thinking of it and got so caught up in his mind until Hakramen shouted with glee and slight trepidation in her voice. "STOPPP!!" she called out.

Bobby realised that even though he had stopped, the plane itself was still growing and growing in front of them until it had almost reached up to the large shelves of the dragon's library.

"It's rather too big now." Hakramen said, standing on the other side of the plane looking up at it. "You really need to practice controlling this mind power of yours Pocromethrah. It seems to run away from you sometimes." Bobby frowned. He was new to this; it wasn't his fault he'd fallen into this world and had left his mum behind. "Mum," thought Bobby. Then he realised why it was so important to find the book he needed.

"Okay fine!" Bobby said, having to close his eyes to get it right in his own head what he wanted to happen. He said it out loud to increase his focus and Hakramen smiled.

"The plane must go to the size big enough for the both of us. I imagine us getting inside it and fitting perfectly." As Bobby concentrated on the words, he recognised himself hearing as Hakramen ran up and into the plane.

"Yes!" she said. Bobby opened his eyes. "Well come on!" she called out to him smiling and sitting in the front seat of the perfectly sized plane. Bobby smiled back. This was exciting, he had never been in a plane like this before and he knew he hadn't created one ever before!

181

Hakramen and Bobby sat in the plane not quite sure what to do next. Bobby turned to his friend.

"How do we fly a plane?" he asked.
"How am I supposed to know?" asked Hakramen.

"Well, what are we supposed to do now then? We haven't got a clue. I mean this button, this button and this button could mean anything!" said Bobby pressing all the buttons in frustration, but what he didn't realise is that the plane was ready to fly and those buttons did mean something.

"Wooah!" cried Bobby as the plane rocked about a bit and suddenly lifted in the air. Hakramen began to panic.

"There must be a lever somewhere!" she called out and looked at Bobby who was now wondering what he could do to help. The plane was moving into the air and it had nothing to guide it.

Suddenly Hakramen stopped and tapped Bobby's shoulder. She pointed to the lever, which for some reason was still as small as the plane had been the first time it had been created.

"Can you grab it?" asked Bobby.
"Wait," said Hakramen trying her hardest to reach the tiny lever below her.

"No. You're going to have to use your powers Bobby. Guide it somehow, guide the plane with your mind. C'mon Pocromethrah!" Hakramen cried out desperately.

Bobby pictured himself guiding the plane to a landing spot up on the shelves. He closed his eyes and panicked in fear as the plane started veering in different directions. Hakramen, who was usually a brave kind of person closed her eyes too. The two of them prayed that something was going to save them from crashing into the shelves.

Even though Bobby was trying as hard as he could in the circumstances, his mind kept getting distracted by the fear of crashing. Suddenly he lost focus and the plane started to quickly lose power and head downwards at a speed.

Amazingly, and to Bobby and Hakramen's surprise, a gust of wind picked the plane up and landed it right in front of a very particular book on the shelf. Bobby read the title, 'THE SECRETS OF SHAMLU'.

"This is the one Dothvera was guarding," said Bobby in wonder, and a little bit of shock from what had just occurred. Bobby thought that if any book would have the translations of Shamlen in it, it would be this one. He smiled knowing he had found the book he needed, but then he looked at the chains and the lock around the book. How was he going to get into this?

Bobby sat in the plane staring at the huge lock on the book. Hakramen decided that it was time to get out and have a look, but Bobby was still mesmerised by what had happened.

"I guess that worked out!" exclaimed Hakramen as she made her way out of the plane. She then grasped the chains around the book and used them to heave herself up beside it.

Once she was at the top, she walked over to the lock and peered into it. "Hmmm," she said curiously as Bobby sat in the plane and watched. "Do you have a huge key?" she called back to Bobby who realised that he should probably join his friend. As he pulled himself up the chains to meet her, he called out, "Of course! I mean that's the kind of thing I keep on me is huge keys, just for situations like this!"

"Okay, okay. I was just wondering if you had seen one or if you knew how to get one? How about a huge paperclip? Can you imagine that into place?"

"Even if I could..." replied Bobby, "...How could we even hold it?" as Bobby and Hakramen stood there looking at the book and working out how to open it, they didn't realise that something was watching them from behind the other large books in the library.

"C'mon Bobby. Don't you think you could dream up a way inside this lock and dream up a way to open it up?"

Bobby didn't really know how locks worked. He didn't realise that inside each lock was a mechanism, that if clicked into place by the correct key, would spring open and release the padlock holding the chains together. He couldn't even imagine how that could work. But just as he was trying to think of a way to imagine the key opening, he saw something glinting in the Shamlen sunlight. It was right there all along, looking like a piece of the library but cleverly hidden in the wall amongst the markings.

"The key!!" Bobby shouted in excitement.

Hakramen looked where Bobby was pointing to. She smiled and ran over to hug her friend. "Yes!" she said.

The two Keepers walked over to the wall in which the key was hidden, and they went to pull at it to retrieve it, but to their surprise the key was actually just a part of the wall. It had no sides which could be held and pulled at to grip at it.

"It must be some kind of dragon magic," said Hakramen. Then Bobby began to read an inscription that was on the key. "Enrusha mio kriah," he said and suddenly the clouds began to roar above him and Hakramen. The key began spinning and spinning and released itself from its place within the wall. Bobby stood staring at it, as it spun itself out of the wall and landed with a clink on the floor in front of them both. Along with it, came a loud roar and Dothvera Ferrucio landed behind them both with a bang. Hakramen and Bobby turned around.

CHAPTER 14

Tongue twisting magic

"Yoooou!" Dothvera roared.

"You dare to steal my book!" the dragon shouted. Then from behind the shadows of the dragon's library, a Boglet appeared and grasped the key in its large black hairy hands. Bobby grasped the other end of the key and pulled. As the Boglet and Bobby fought in a tug of war, Hakramen jumped in and attacked the Boglet with her sword. But before she could, the Boglet disappeared with the key.

Dothvera lowered his head and roared in despair.

"Noooooooo!" called out the dragon so loudly that it shook the whole of Shamlu.

Bobby looked up at Dothvera who was clearly in distress about what had just happened. "I can help," he said looking into the dragon's sad eyes. "I can imagine this back into place."

Dothvera looked at the boy, "That was Amelia's key. She created it and only she could retrieve it. She kept it hidden all those years and now..." Dothvera Ferrucio lowered his head, "...because I feared this, it has happened." The dragon walked away his head low and his usually proud and confident self diminishing.

"But the book is still here," Bobby called out after him. Suddenly the dragons head appeared very closely to the boy's face. He had turned his neck and stretched it far out to reach Bobby.

"It's not about the book Bobby, it's about fear. I feared that would happen and it did. I did this. I Dothvera Ferrucio. Amelia's most trusted dragon and confidant. I lost her key, something which seemed impossible because no one could access the key except for her. Something seemingly impossible happened because I feared it. That Boglet came for me." Bobby heard the right words appear in his mind and began speaking to the dragon as though he knew exactly what to say.

"But it isn't impossible, because I just made the impossible possible, which means whatever you fear. Whatever you think you cannot defeat because you think it's impossible, is no longer to be feared, because I am here and I will make the impossible happen." Bobby couldn't believe what just came out of his own mouth, but he had said it and Dothvera bowed his head down respectfully. His friend Pocromethrah had just appeared and spoken to him for the first time.

"Indeed. You are right and wise to say so, Pocromethrah." Dothvera Ferrucio answered and then the dragon flew away and upon his leaving, the book opened itself to the page that Bobby had been searching for: READING SHAMLEN. But the page was far smaller a page than Bobby had thought it to be. The only words Amelia had written were: If you are at this page, you can already read Shamlen. Bobby sighed and sat down where he was. Hakramen read the page and sat next to Bobby.

"Oh," she said.
"I don't get it." replied Bobby.
"The key!!" Hakramen called out, "You read the key on the wall, how did you do that?"
Bobby realised that he did. "Of course!" he said.
"But I didn't know what it meant,"
"Didn't you? Do you remember it?"
"Yeah it said… um. Open my key!"

Bobby couldn't believe what he had just heard himself say, "I mean, it said um… Open my key. It said open my key. Open my key. Oooopppeeenn mmmmyyyy kkkeeeeeyyyy."

No matter how Bobby tried he couldn't seem to say what he was meaning to. The words were coming out in English, but he was saying the words in Shamlen. As if by magic, each word was translating itself and he could feel it being translated onto his tongue, like the words were changing without him doing anything to change them.

"Yes, I heard you the first time!"
"No, but I didn't say that the first time. I didn't say open my key. I said open my key!" said Bobby trying to get the message across as best as he could.

Hakramen stared at Bobby in confusion.

"Yes, I know!" the poor woman replied.
"No, you don't get it. I'm not saying open my key. I'm trying to say open my key, but I'm not saying open my key, because I can't say what I read in Shamlen."

Hakramen was sure that her friend had completely lost the plot by now. Bobby jumped up and down. "It said OPEN MY KEY, OPEN MY KEY THAT'S WHAT IT SAID!" the boy exclaimed loudly and laughing to himself. Now he could definitely translate Shamlen.

"So, okay I get it! Let's get back to the book then." said Hakramen.

"But what about this book? How do we lock it again?"

"I'm not sure." answered Hakramen, walking away.

"Hakramen. Come on, we need to lock it." said Bobby following his friend as she walked down the open book pages as though they were a large set of steps, but the pair of them didn't have to work anything out. For as soon as they stepped off the book, it snapped shut and the lock clamped back into place immediately.

"Well, that's that sorted." said Hakramen and they headed towards the Plane.

Inside the plane, Hakramen was quiet.

"Everything okay?" Bobby asked, curious as to why she was not quite as excited as before.

"Yes." answered Hakramen. Bobby thought for a moment why his friend was feeling differently. Was it something he had said?

"Was it something I said?" he asked.

"I just don't know why you kept repeating the same sentence over and over and over, as if I knew what you were on about. I honestly don't have a clue what just happened."

"Ohhhhh," replied Bobby suddenly realising.

"Well I can try and explain it, but it might not make any sense." he continued.

"Not much here does make sense I suppose." she replied.

"Okay well, here's what happened. I was trying to tell you what the words said in Shamlen, but um… I couldn't."

"What do you mean?"

"I couldn't because I kept saying the words in English instead. It was like magic. The Shamlen words appeared in my head and when I said them, I spoke them in English!" even upon repeating what had happened, Bobby was still in shock.

"You mean, you couldn't say those words in Shamlen??"

"No!"

"Wow!" said Hakramen, the light suddenly flooding into her eyes again.

"So you are now a translator of Shamlen too?"

"I guess so." answered Bobby.

"Then you'll have no problem reading what your grandfather wrote on Amelia's map then?"

"Probably not."

"Then I guess you know all the secrets of Shamlu."

"I guess," answered Bobby. Now that he was realising that he was closer to getting home, a strange sense of sadness came over the boy.

Yes, of course he wanted to see his mother, but he didn't want to leave Shamlu for good. Did he? Bobby began thinking about everything that had happened so far. The moment he had entered this place and everyone he had met. He thought about the dragons, the unicorns, the beautiful skies, the towers that had begun to feel like his home. Most of all, he thought about Dothvera Ferrucio who had protected and cared for him all along.

"Here we are," said Hakramen, safely bringing the plane to a halt. "That was a lot quicker on the way back eh?" she smiled.

"Mm." he answered in acknowledgement.

Bobby and Hakramen walked up to the page where the map was left open. He read the words written on the edge of the map. 'In between.' and 'Remember.'

"So, what do they say?"

"That is 'in between' and there where the arrows point outwards is called 'remember'" Bobby said pointing to the spaces on the map.

"Remember??" questioned Hakramen and as soon as she said it, Bobby realised what the word 'Remember' must have meant.

"Home!" he said. "That's home!"

Bobby's eyes suddenly lit up and he thought about how wonderful it would be to see his mum and to hold her tight. Upon seeing this, it suddenly hit Hakramen that the boy's intention had not been just to study that day.

"You're trying to get HOME!" called out Hakramen.
"Well, Um, No, I…, What do you mean?"

"That's why you said you 'needed' this. You just want to leave us all here and leave us to save ourselves. You can't be Pocromethrah! He wouldn't leave us, not now!" Bobby wasn't quite sure why Hakramen was so upset. He only wanted to see his mother and show her that he was safe and well. He thought he had been away for weeks.

"I…" Bobby paused, "No! Hakramen!" he called out after his friend as she proceeded to walk away from the dragon's library. Bobby tried to control the fear that was now rushing through his mind. Hakramen was sure to inform the dragons now.

As Hakramen ran off and tried to work out what she was going to do, Bobby decided to call upon Dothvera Ferrucio. Maybe this was time to come clean.

"Dothvera Ferrucio!!!" he called up into the skies, "DOTHVERA FERRUCIO!!" The dragon hearing his calls clearly, swept down through the skies to the dragon's library and landed in the human sized library crushing the plane on his arrival.

"Yes Lad." the dragon said.

"I'm sorry." said Bobby lowering his head.

"For what?" asked Dothvera.

"I failed you. I know you are training me to be this great and powerful person, but I just want to go home and see my mum and now I think I know where home is. I just want to go back."

"I know." said Dothvera, to Bobby's surprise.

"But…"

"And it's okay, as we said. We'll take you when you're ready." said Dothvera not giving away that he really knew that Bobby was working on a proper plan and happy that the boy felt he needed to explain and that he was honest after all.

"It's okay Bobby, here's my advice though. Before you return, make sure you remember to read Chapter seventeen of your grandfather's journal. I believe he gave it to you before he left.

Go to page three and a half. It explains who we think you are going to be and it's written in dragons' ink, so you might need this to help you find it." The dragon breathed into a tiny bottle and tied it to a string that he hung around Bobby's neck. The warmth of the bottle filled with dragon's breath warmed Bobby up all over like a hot water bottle.

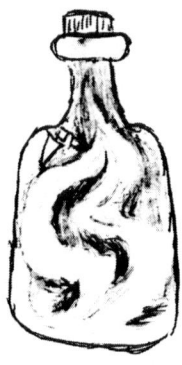

Bobby picked up the tiny bottle and stared at it in amazement. Inside was a tiny captured piece of dragon's breath, like a small fiery globule that was moving around in the bottle. Bobby wondered what on earth he would need it for, but he tried to remember the numbers chapter seventeen and page three and a half. Maybe it would come in useful sometime. The dragon then prepared himself for take-off.

"Wait!" Dothvera stopped, "Before you leave, I have some questions." the dragon nodded. He liked these moments of teaching the young lad.
"Indeed. Go ahead Pocromethrah." Dothvera winked at Bobby.

"How come you said you couldn't leave the books and here you can? And how could I not read Shamlen one moment and after saying 'open my key' I could? And...."
"One at a time."

197

"Okay." Bobby said.

"So, here are my answers: Here in Shamlu, part of my animal spirit is tied to the books and the same happens in between Shamlu and your home. As an ornament to protect the words of Amelia, I am always sat on the books. Here, I am warned. I can sense if anyone touches the books."

"So? you knew?"

"I knew what?"

"That we were on the book earlier?"

"Yes, so I came closer to inspect, but I didn't think you would find your way inside. The key you found is precious. It opens all the secrets of Shamlu to whoever frees it. Before you, only your grandmother had even known of the key and used it."

"So, what will the Boglet do with it?"

"The Boglet cannot speak. Boglets are only harmful because of what they represent. My fear lost us the key. I am just upset that it was stolen, it was so precious and held many memories of Amelia for me and for all the dragons."

"So, because I freed it, it opened the secrets of Shamlu into my mind, which is why I knew how to translate Shamlen?

"Indeed."

"So, what exactly is the Black Dragon and why is everyone so afraid of it Dothvera?"

Dothvera Ferrucio felt a deep fear within him at the very words 'Black Dragon' but he knew now was the best time to speak. Before Bobby found his way home, he needed to learn the truth.

"The Black Dragon of Dahkrath is a fearsome creature. It became worse and worse as Amelia tried to protect our world from it, and all the creatures of Dahkrath. Your grandmother created a magic and banished the Black Dragon to Dahkrath past the Dahk Velar (the Dark Sea) and there he torments and kills all in his path. Amelia has protected us and built a wall of magic that could keep it from us, and it has worked for a long time. However, there is talk of a time when Amelia's magic will weaken, and things will change."

"And you think I can help?" asked Bobby nervously.

"Maybe. Just read Chapter seventeen page three and a half of your grandfather's journal when you get home, yes? Promise me?"
Bobby promised.

"Now there is more training to complete. Come with me."

CHAPTER 15

Love and Fear
Lomorrah a Destruccio

Now that word had got out that Bobby had unlocked the key, the dragons knew he would soon be finding his way back home. They didn't realise it would be this soon, but now they had to try and complete their training in an even shorter space of time.

"Do you think he is the one in the prophecy Dothvera Cherama?"

"I believe he is." answered the oldest and wisest dragon.

"I hope so." answered Dothvera Ferrucio. "Or all is lost," they said, but only in their own minds. Now that Bobby could translate Shamlen and had opened the key, they had to be extra careful about what they said around him.

"Pocromethrah?" asked Dothvera Cherama, the boy looked up and into the dragon's ancient eyes. "Since you have opened the key to Shamlen's secrets, you no longer need to be trained in the ways of Shamlu or its language. Now we need to begin the lessons in facing fear and building courage within you. It is time to begin."

Bobby nodded and the dragons decided amongst themselves what was the best thing to do next. Now they had to get the boy to be able to focus on his imagination and create under pressure.

"First lesson: Travelling." 'Travelling?' Bobby thought. What could that be?

"We need you to travel from one place to another, simply using your mind. So, we will place you on the top of this mountain here and we want you to take yourself to Dothvera Ferrucio using your mind."

Bobby just stared at Dothvera Cherama as if he were speaking gobbeldy-gook. The dragon smiled to see the shock on the child's face. He was glad to be challenging Bobby's beliefs. This was what mind training was all about.

"Okay," said Dothvera Cherama ignoring Bobby's expression. "We are going to stay here until you have completed this task today Pocromethrah. This is an important lesson and it will serve you well. Just try it for me, okay? You can close your eyes for this one if you need to." The dragon patted Bobby on the shoulder with the tip of his wing and flew up to the top of the other mountains to watch what was going to happen. Dothvera Cherama knew he was asking a lot from the boy. After all this was quite a task. It had taken Amelia a long time to discover that she could do this. Even when she had done it by accident to escape a danger, she still hadn't quite got around to believing it.

"But what do I DO??" panicked Bobby who was standing on top of the mountain, more confused than ever.

"Imagine Bobby, just imagine," Dothvera Cherama said encouragingly.

Bobby stood there nervously. "Imagine," he thought to himself. "Imagine. What would Amelia do? What would Grandpa do?" Bobby suddenly remembered what he had done to create the plane. "Believe, Focus, Let go." he thought. "Believe, Focus, Let go," he said aloud. "BELIEVE. FOCUS. LET GO."

Bobby tried to picture himself, appearing on Dothvera Ferrucio's wing and what that would feel like. He tried to make it as clear as he could. He felt the breeze in his mind. But he then heard something rustling in the bushes behind him.

Bobby turned around. Whatever this was, it didn't look very friendly. It was a large pig like creature with huge teeth and a red snout. It took one look at Bobby and started to scoop its hooves into the dirt below, as if it was about to charge towards him.

Bobby closed his eyes and desperately believed that he could get out of here but on opening them, he was faced with the creature again. Bobby kept saying the words aloud. Fear almost distracting him away from his task. Then he heard the sounds of the dragons. "Believe. Focus. Let go." they chanted louder and louder. Bobby tried to focus his mind. He did believe more things were possible, he was more and more focused now. All he had to do was...

"Well done, congratulations," applauded the dragons. Bobby opened his eyes, which he had closed in panic as the last thing he had seen was the image of the frightening creature heading towards him. Bobby tried to work out what exactly he had done. He was actually sitting on Dothvera Ferrucio's head right now and he wanted to know what had got him this far. Letting go seemed to be the hardest part of the three rules to creating.

Bobby struggled to believe sometimes, but he was finding it easier these days after all the impossible things he had done. Focusing wasn't always easy, but in the face of something fearful, Bobby found his focus became much sharper. But letting go and just letting the whole thing happen was the scariest because it was the final bit of the puzzle. It was also the bit that meant that Bobby had to succeed and that was the hardest bit of all, because Bobby was so scared of not succeeding.

"You know that everyone is afraid a little Bobby," said Dothvera Ferrucio sensing the boy's thoughts. The boy looked up and wondered what it was that made this dragon so wise.

"Can you always hear my thoughts Dothvera?" asked Bobby.
"It's a gift but I don't always need to use it, but I sense fear mostly, the fear that you won't make it

back home, the fear that you won't be good enough to do all you have to do, the fear that you aren't strong enough to defeat the Black Dragon. I feel it within you often, but I felt it within Amelia, I felt it within your grandfather and I feel it within the dragons themselves. Everyone is afraid in some way Bobby, but it is overcoming that fear which is the bravest thing of all,"

"You think so?" asked Bobby.
"Indeed,"
"Dothvera?"
"Yes,"

"What do you think my great grandmother meant when she said that love can destroy fear, how does that work?"

"Well, in my eyes, I think it means that to love is the bravest thing you can do. It's easy to fear things, Bobby, but it's not always easy to love things. It's easy to get angry when you feel fear but it is not easy to give yourself love when you are fearful. However, the bravest thing you can do is show love in the face of fear. For fear cannot exist in the same space as love."

"But how can I love my fear, my fear is what stops me from being brave?"
"No, your fear is what makes you brave my boy. Fear is what teaches you bravery and courage.

Without feeling fear, you cannot know what to do to feel courageous and be strong."

"I'm afraid of the Black Dragon Dothvera,"
"So am I,"
"You are?" Bobby said in shock.

He was sure that nothing could make such a brilliant and brave creature such as Dothvera Ferrucio afraid. It suddenly came to the boy that when he had created an image of another dragon in front of this brave dragon, he had seen fear in Dothvera's eyes. It was the kind of fear that even a wonderful dragon like Dothvera Ferrucio could not hide.

"We are all afraid of something," replied the dragon.
"Time for your next travelling challenge Pocromethrah," interrupted Dothvera Cherama.
"Now you must learn to transfer yourself onto a moving target."

Bobby took a deep breath.

"So, what did you learn today?"

Reikiila asked Bobby, who was back in the dragon's library studying fear and love and their powers in Shamlu.

"Dragon Jumping mainly," answered the boy as if it was just a normal day at training that he had been to.

"Dragon Jumping?" asked Reikiila. "Did you do it?" this was the first time that Reikiila had shown any interest in what Bobby was doing with the dragons every day.

"I did, after the tenth attempt, I almost landed in the air, but Dothvera Velara caught me with his water and landed me back safely onto the ground. That was a bit scary!" Reikiila's face dropped at the thought of it.

"Yes, I imagine it would be. So how is your imagining going? Are you finding it easier?"

Bobby responded by holding out his hand. A saucer appeared in his palm, then a cup to go in the saucer and then it filled with tea, which he offered to the older man who seemed utterly amazed.

"Sugar?" asked Bobby confidently.
"Impressive. Unfortunately I don't drink tea," answered Reikiila, "but I am impressed,"

"I do!" answered Hakramen and took the teacup from Bobby smiling. Bobby was glad to see his friend again and glad that she was smiling this time.

Hakramen took one sip of the tea and spat it out right in front of Reikiila almost spraying him.

"No sugar!" she said, "Eugh!"
Bobby created a square of sugar for Hakramen and dropped it in her tea. Then he realised she needed a spoon and he created one and began stirring the tea as she held it.

"Awwesssomme!" said Hakramen and Reikiila walked away.

Bobby decided to ask Hakramen about what had happened last time she had seen him, but he didn't quite know how to approach the situation.

"Hey," he said.
"Hey!" she replied.
"Um." they both said at the same time and then laughed at the coincidence of it.

"I just hope you realise that we need you to come back," said Hakramen, who had decided to keep their last conversation to herself.

"I know." said Bobby. He knew everyone was relying on him, but he was scared that he couldn't bring them the thing they needed, peace in Shamlen.

As the two of them continued to chat, they were completely unaware that a dark force was beginning to seep out of the magic wall that Amelia had built, but the dragons could feel it.

"We have seen more Boglets appearing in Shamlu" said Dothvera Ferrucio. "One appeared to me only recently and Bobby has seen one. Also I had word that Reikiila saw a Boglet too, that took the shape of the Black Dragon. He is afraid that it is a sign,"

CHAPTER 15

"Amelia's magic must be losing its power," answered Dothvera Cherama.

"Brothers," he said, addressing all the dragons, who were up at the highest and furthest point in the skies of Shamlu to keep curious ears from hearing them. The dragons gathered together to hear Dothvera Cherama's words. "We must keep our eyes upon the wall of magic and Dahkrath, there appears to be a break in the wall and things are escaping. Our job is to protect our world and the lands above and below us, keep a look out and report anything suspicious to me, Darmapetth has begun."

As the dragon spoke, deep in the skies of Dahkrath, something evil was listening. The Black Dragon had been waiting for this moment. It was his time, and he was not going to let it go to waste. Darmapetth was close now and he knew it.

As the Black Dragon moved eerily through the black skies, the magical wall was showing signs of wear and tear. The magical streams of light that had once shone upon the wall was starting to dull and it was beginning to look old and worn, nothing like Amelia had created it to be. Small gaps of dullness and grey spots were appearing in it and its magic was clearly beginning to fail. Soon the darkness would take over again. Soon, the Black Dragon would be free.

Back in the dragon's library, Bobby explained to Hakramen what he had learned about fear and love and what their powers were in Shamlu.

"So, fear is a creative force and so is love, but one cancels out the other. Their powers are equal, and so what Amelia says is that fear is an enemy because it creates itself in Shamlu,"

"Creates itself?" asked Hakramen.

"Yes, listen to this, 'whenever I have the feeling of fear it seems to take control of me in here and grow and become something terrible. I have noticed it many times. It seems that my fear of the Black Dragon is too strong and it torments me on a daily basis. I don't know how to do this but I believe that love has a power that could overcome it. But love of what? I do not love the Black Dragon. I cannot. It is evil. Though whenever I love anything here, it treats me with a love of an equal force. I have had creatures protect me and spend time caring for me in times of grave danger. It appears my love for these creatures makes them what they are, loving and brave. It appears all my feelings, good or bad, are doubled and tripled here.'

"You see what I mean?"
"Amelia wrote that?"
"Yes."

"But I don't know how we can use that to destroy the Black Dragon and all its evil creatures and Dahkrath," said Hakramen.

"No, I know, but it's interesting isn't it?" said Bobby.

"Have you found out about the magic wall of Dahkrath? Maybe you could find out how Amelia made it,"
"It says that she just imagined it into place, but she knew there would be a time when it was not needed."

"Not needed, the protective wall of Dahkrath? Not needed?" quizzed Hakramen, feeling confused. "What could that mean? Of course, it's needed. It protects everything here,"

"Yes, I know, I'll have to think about it. But first I need to get myself home Hakramen, I need to get my grandfather's journal and I think getting myself home somehow is part of how I get back and save everyone."

"You do?"
"Yes, maybe there's something I need, something I've missed, something of my grandfathers I can use,"

"Well, his journal might actually be one of the best things you can have. It was a detailed

212

account of his journeys here and it had millions of pages. All that Sir Robert ever learned was in there. Do you think you have it?"

"I think I do," Bobby said, smiling.

Bobby had been given a journal by his grandfather which he had left to him in his will. Bobby did think it strange that his grandfather would leave him an old notebook with nothing in it but blank pages. He could have got one of them anywhere.

Now that he was thinking about it, it had to be the thing everyone had mentioned to him. If dragon's ink was only visible in Shamlu then of course Bobby wouldn't have seen that it was his grandfather's journal. Bobby hoped he was right. He knew he had to get back home, hug his mum, get that journal and bring it back to Shamlu to read it through.

Now he just needed a good plan.

CHAPTER 16

Getting home

"Will you help me Hakramen?" Bobby asked, realising that he might need someone to help him get back home. The Keeper nodded. But before the pair of them could begin, they were interrupted by Reikiila and Totomal.

"Traitor!" yelled Reikiila at Hakramen. Hakramen stood ready to fight but Bobby stood in front of her.
"Wait." said Bobby.

"You think I'm going to listen to a kid like you, Totomal get her." Reikiila commanded. Totomal walked up to Hakramen and Bobby panicked.

"No! Stop!" he yelled, putting his hand out and to his surprise Totomal and Reikiila felt their feet hold them to the floor so that all they could do was stand absolutely still where they were.

214

"Remove your curse from us at once!" said Reikiila, who couldn't move a bone in his body.

"Only if I can guarantee that you do not fight us and help us instead." demanded Bobby, who wasn't sure what exactly he had done to the two Keepers.

Reikiila and Totomal stood their ground, but after over an hour had passed with the two of them standing in the same place and not being able to move, Totomal finally gave in.

"Okay," he said to Bobby and Hakramen who had decided to continue and ignore the pair of Keepers, whilst trying to work out a plan.

Without Bobby moving from his seat, Totomal was freed. Reikiila looked on in shock as he continued to be held prisoner in his own body. Bobby approached Reikiila and spoke to the weary old man who was now tired and worn out from standing for so long.

"Listen to me Reikiila. I know that you don't like me. You don't have to like me, but I need to get back and get to my grandfather's journal to find out what messages there are inside. I promise you, on the life of everything in Shamlu, I will return and I will protect you all as best as I can."

As Reikiila stood there a tear fell down his eye, and out of nowhere in that very moment a Boglet appeared. It stared at Reikiila and left behind it an image of the Keeper lying dead on the floor in front of himself. Bobby felt sad for Reikiila and in that moment the Keeper fell to the floor and onto his knees deep in fear of his own ending.

Bobby walked over to the image and imagined it gone. As it slowly disappeared, he picked Reikiila up and held his shoulders and looked him in the eye warrior to warrior.

"Reikiila. You need to trust me now, and I need to trust you." the Keeper nodded, tears rolling down his cheeks. Bobby, who had never felt so sure of himself before, hugged the old man and held him tight as Reikiila poured out his fear and left it in the past.

"Okay." said Bobby finally in front of all three Keepers. "Let's find out how I get home."

The Keepers stood in front of Bobby wondering what kind of plan he was going to come up with. For the first time in a long while, Bobby felt nervous about what was ahead. He didn't know how he could get home; he didn't know if his power would take him back home. All he knew was that if he were to succeed, he would have to make his way back to his world and find his grandfather's journal.

Now was the time to start a plan. But what plan?

"Does anyone have any idea what I might be able to do?" asked Bobby. The Keepers looked a bit lost at first, but Reikiila answered eventually.

"Why don't we all go through the books in this library and see if there is something that we can find that might help you."

"That's a great idea!" Bobby answered, not expecting Reikiila to have been the first one to help him out. The Keepers all walked up to the library and grabbed a book each.

Bobby followed them.

For the first time he was feeling like the person he imagined Pocromethrah to be. The Keepers were listening to him and helping him. Bobby felt like they were finally respecting him for the person he was becoming. It was frightening but thrilling at the same time. Now all they had to do was devise a plan.

The Keepers sat at the library desk their heads in different books. Reikiila was reading 'Listening to dragons' written by Amelia. Hakramen was reading 'The art of Shamlen's creation' written by Sir Robert. Totomal was reading a book about the lands of Shamlu and Bobby was reading a book about 'imagining'. It was a book written by his grandmother and Dothvera Cherama together. As Bobby read about how imagining was a skill that took courage and a dedicated focus, he was interrupted by Hakramen.

"Take a look at this!" she said, putting the book in front of Bobby. Bobby read as Hakramen underlined the sentences with her finger.

'Creating is a practice. An art if you like. Many times I have tried and failed, but when deciding what you want, rather than worrying about what the plan is, just decide on a way and imagine it. Shamlu is a magical place and it can give you anything you desire. Just work out a way. It doesn't matter which way. All paths lead to what you want. Just follow one and trust that it is the right one and it WILL BE.' Bobby sat still for a moment. Then he closed Hakramen's book and the book he was reading.

"We're overthinking it!" he exclaimed. Suddenly realising what he must do.

"What?" asked Reikiila thinking the boy must be mad.

"Close your books. We're trying to work out something as if we were back in our world. I was wrong. We must use our imaginations." Reikiila continued to read his book in a bid to prove Bobby wrong. Bobby ignored Reikiila's response and looked at the other Keepers.

"Totomal? Hakramen?" he asked, looking at the others. Hakramen put down her book and started to think.

"How about we fly you to the edge of Shamlu and then you try and walk through? Or you could create your own Key! Or..."

"What if you don't need a key?" said Totomal suddenly. Reikiila looked up in wonder. "What if the reason why you fell in here so easily is because YOU ARE THE KEY." The room fell silent for a moment.

"Totomal you utter genius!" said Bobby in amazement, realising how right that sounded. It made complete sense that if Bobby fell into the world without a Key, which all Keepers had, except for Amelia, then he was likely already a

219

key to the world of Shamlu. He was the key. Of course he was.

That was why he fell in here, that was why he was treated the way he was by the dragons. That is why he was such an asset to the world of Shamlu and that was how he was going to fall back out.

"So how do we get there?" asked Hakramen.

"I know how. We follow the map." answered Bobby, as he went to find the exact book where he had found the original map. Bobby laid Amelia's journal out and then he opened the map. Reikiila, Hakramen, Totomal and Bobby leaned in to see the map in its entirety.

Bobby translated.

"This here is the 'in between'. This is Ye Olde Ornamental Shop, where things come to life. This here is marked 'remember' and that means it is home." The Keepers couldn't believe their eyes. None of them had seen anyone translate Shamlen before except for Hakramen, and even she was enjoying how amazing it was to see Bobby's skills growing every day.

"So, where are we?" asked Reikiila. It was a good question.

Bobby studied the map. He saw the mountain range where he was training with the dragons. He saw Dahkrath at the other edge of the map. He saw names of the outer lands. He couldn't however find out where he was. He couldn't find the towers on the map.

"I guess they weren't built back when this was drawn," said Bobby nervously. That was where he spent most of his time and where he could meet the Keepers. The dragons had never left him around by the mountains. This was seeming trickier and trickier to work out.

"What if we ask the dragons to train us together?" Hakramen asked, "Maybe we can ask them to teach us similar things?"

"Oh yes, of course…" interrupted Reikiila again with his usual approach, "…because you and I are both masters of our minds," he said sarcastically. Hakramen stared at him angrily.

"It was a good suggestion Hakramen, I think we could just write down suggestions and find one that we can all agree on." said Bobby, trying to keep the peace amongst the Keepers, which even he had to admit wasn't the easiest of tasks.

Reikiila, though quite insulting and awfully rude and hard to get along with most of the time, was wise at times and could really make points that were valid. Totomal, the quietest of the group only spoke when he had something useful to say. He was the most reserved, yet most calculated with his communication and Hakramen was gentle, fun and came up with the wildest ideas. Although they sometimes seemed impossible and crazy even Bobby had to admit, they were sometimes pure genius.

Putting everyone together was the important thing. They were actually a great team that balanced one another out and Bobby, being slightly crazier than Totomal and Reikiila but slightly less mercurial than Hakramen, fitted perfectly in the middle as the reasoner of the group.

"I think we should all take a piece of paper." said Bobby drawing up pieces of paper in his mind that drifted in front of each keeper, "...and a pen," said Bobby getting actual ballpoint pens for everyone that landed perfectly next to the pieces of paper, "...then we can just quietly and anonymously write things down. Then I can take a look and mix them up. Then we can choose fairly."

The Keepers began scribbling ideas down on their pieces of paper.

Hakramen had that wicked look in her eye as she imagined up all kinds of crazy ideas. Reikiila was watching everyone else for moments and then in between that he was coming up with ideas and sneakily writing them down before watching everyone else again to see what they were all up to. Totomal didn't write much at all but sat quietly and still while he pondered the question in his mind.

Bobby felt like a teacher in a classroom. He almost wanted to make a joke and say 'hand in your papers, class dismissed' to everyone at the end, but he didn't think that everyone in the room would find it funny. Still, the boy chuckled to himself in his own head about the situation. Even Reikiila was paying attention.

"Aren't you going to write anything?" asked Reikiila.
"I will when I think of an idea." answered Bobby.

"He's not all that good at ideas. I've got so many I'm bursting open with them, but I think Pocromethrah is more of a creator than an ideas guy." interrupted Hakramen.

Bobby was going to stand up for himself, but he soon realised that Hakramen probably had a point. She wasn't being mean; it was true that Bobby struggled to come up with ideas. Plus, he was so busy trying to focus his mind all the time to create what people asked for, that it wasn't something he could do easily.

"It's a bit true actually," said Bobby to everyone there, "I'm not all that good at coming up with ideas. That's why I need you. You are all good at coming up with ideas. Hakramen, you are... crazy but also brilliant minded at the same time. Reikiila, you are the rudest person I know, but you have experience and that counts for something and Totomal, I have never heard such wise words spoken. You are calculated and sure about what you say. I, however, I am just a boy that has no clue about what life is actually like. I don't know what it's like to fight battles here in Shamlu or in my own world. I was always imaginative because of my grandfather and what he used to tell me, but I mainly have one power and it only exists here. I can create things with focused effort, and I hope I can create something that can save Shamlu and all who are here."

The Keepers went quiet for a moment, trying to take in all that Bobby had said. Reikiila realised that Bobby, although he was considered this great person and although he was a great and highly skilled imaginer, was also just a boy. A boy with a great responsibility placed upon him. Reikiila was busy playing in school yards at that age. He hadn't been expected to save a world at ten years old. Suddenly, the old man felt a sincere kindness towards Bobby.

Pocromethrah, the person that the boy would become, would be expected to do great things and he would need the support of those around him in order to do those great things.

"I think that is the reason why we are here beside you Pocromethrah. To stand by your side and support all that you are, despite what I may have said. I love this world and all that is in it. I love Dothvera Velara. I love these Keepers and I do not want to see it all destroyed."

Hakramen walked over to Reikiila and hugged him tightly. The old man looked awkward as she grabbed onto him and squeezed him with love. Reikiila was not used to being like that with anyone. Not even his father or mother were the kind of people to hug him. But even he felt a warm glow inside his heart when Hakramen did what she did. Maybe things were beginning to change for the old man.

"I have an idea." said Totomal proudly and everyone turned to listen.

"I have heard that you created a flying contraption once before. So, if you can create one that is invisible to the eye, we can follow the dragons to the training grounds and map a route there along the way. Then when we return we can take you to the training grounds when the dragons drop you off in the library to study, and we can fly over to the edge of Shamlu and see that you get home safely." The Keepers all smiled at Totomal's idea. Then they turned to Bobby.

"Sounds great!" said Bobby, "I just need to work on creating a plane that is big enough for all of us and that is um... invisible." the boy said, not quite sure how he was going to do this, but liking the sound of the idea.

CHAPTER 17

Tiny keepers and big ears

Bobby didn't want the plane that he was going to create to be like the last one. For one thing, he had to be able to create something that was the right size all the way through. He also wanted to be able to create a good level of invisibility. He decided to read up on invisibility in Shamlu, to see whether Amelia Bobcat had ever tried anything like that before.

He knew that this process might take a while. He hadn't trained himself to create the first plane. He knew that this one was going to take some time. However, there were several elements that he hadn't practiced before. Such as the size of the plane, the fact that it needed to be invisible to the dragons and the fact that it had to be much easier to fly than the last one. In this plane, everything had to be a much more manageable size. Bobby couldn't make any mistakes this time. This plane had to be perfect.

Bobby headed to the library to find a book on creating things that he could study to remind himself of the process. Just as he entered the room, he saw the dragons there looking at the books that were already out on the table. Bobby panicked. Were the dragons trying to find out what he was doing? He didn't want to be caught out now. He entered the room and looked up at the dragons.

"Is it time for my training?" Bobby called upwards, hoping to distract them. The dragons looked down towards Bobby.
"Ahhh, Pocromethrah." said Dothvera Cherama.

"I'm ready for training if you are," answered the boy. The dragons, aware that Bobby was nervous, stopped what they were doing and spoke to the boy.

"Is everything okay my lad?" asked Dothvera Cherama.
"Yes, I'm just wondering what you are looking for?"
"Some Boglets appeared here the other day and we wanted to know what they were doing?" answered Dothvera Ferrucio.

"Oh?" said Bobby realising that probably made sense.

"Yes, so training will be a little bit later. You are free to use the library though Pocromethrah." said Dothvera Cherama. "We will depart the human section," he continued and stepped away from the human library so that Bobby could study.

Bobby was beginning to worry about the dragons.

They were bound to find out what he was doing eventually. What if they caught him making the plane? What if it wasn't invisible to dragons but it was invisible to humans? He would have to put this to the test. What if he couldn't do this in time? What if his mother had already forgotten him? A million thoughts rushed into his mind.

Bobby tried to put those thoughts to rest. He looked for a book about creating larger objects like planes. He decided the best thing to do was to find every book on creating that he could, and start there. Bobby started to pile up the books. Anything that had the word 'creating' in the title he added to the selection of books on the table.

Bobby had to get good at creating things in Shamlu. This had to be all he practiced from now on. He couldn't let the Keepers down. He couldn't let his mum down and most of all, he couldn't let himself down. It was now or never.

Bobby decided the best time to practice his skills was in his room when the dragons took him back there for a sleep. At least there, he could practice in silence and hopefully not disturb the dragons' while they slept. Tonight, he would begin. But first he would need to read up on the creation process. Had anyone ever tried to create a plane in this world? If they had, how had they gone about it? How could he do it successfully this time around so that it didn't fail as it had last time?

Bobby walked over to the shelves and scanned them. Now that the dragons had left, he could continue to look for the books he needed. Creating things wasn't something that had been written about by everyone.

Most of the books on that subject were there because Amelia had taken time to write them. 'The Art of Shamlen Creation' was a particularly interesting book that was written about Amelia, and how she had created everything in this world. The book that Bobby had been reading earlier, which was simply called 'Imagining' was a book also written by Amelia about the imagination process. These were the two main books that Bobby could read.

As Bobby scanned through 'The Art of Shamlen Creation' he noticed that Amelia had created all kinds of things. These included the magical wall and the dragons. Then he came across something that made him wonder.

Amelia had created the ways in and out of Shamlu. She had made Dothvera into a doorway dragon and she had created a second version of him. He had become the first of his kind. Amelia had created the actual doorways to this world. Is that how she got back home the first time? Had she created the doorways and then just used them, as if she was building a door to a house and then just went through the door?

Bobby wondered if this was possible for him. Could he just decide on a way out and then go?

He wasn't sure if the Keepers would understand this idea. They were, particularly Reikiila and Totomal, completely unsure about anything a little bit different to the rules of their own world. They didn't really understand that in this world, and for someone like Bobby, anything really WAS possible. Maybe Bobby would just follow the path the way he had planned it.

Scanning further, Bobby could see that no one had ever tried to create a plane in the world of Shamlu. However, Amelia had once created herself to become invisible. This was to escape the eyes of the Black Dragon and to build the magic wall that separated Dahkrath from Shamlu, but the magic had almost worn off and she had almost been caught. This was because she had noticed the dragon beginning to sense her presence and amazingly she had escaped his wrath with only moments to spare. The story had really captured Bobby's imagination.

Bobby hoped his invisibility creation would be a lot stronger than Amelia's. He was thinking he might put a time limit on it, but then he realised that time wasn't valid in Shamlu. Time didn't seem to exist here. It was vital that Bobby worked on the invisibility of his plane and created it to make sure it lasted at least a day.

But how long was a day in Shamlu? Bobby had no idea. This was going to be a problem for him.

Bobby decided the next thing he had to do was to put this to the test. Maybe if he created a smaller plane to begin with, something that was so small it could be completely missed by the dragons. Then a crazy idea came into his mind. What if he could do that? This required a meeting with the Keepers.

Bobby stood in front of the Keepers whom he had gathered to tell them his crazy new plan.

"So, I thought it might be a good idea to ask you this, because I have found out that invisibility spells do not really last and well, I would like to get us all through this safely, so I have thought of something..."

Bobby looked into the eyes of all the Keepers. Reikiila's face was saying it all. He probably wasn't going to like this one. Hakramen would probably just go along with it because it sounded fun and Totomal, well Bobby wasn't sure if Totomal would understand it completely.

"Okay" said Bobby taking a deep breath in anticipation of sharing his idea.

"I think we should fly in a miniature plane." the boy said.

"A miniature plane, but that means we would have to be..."
"Miniature, yes." Bobby answered Reikiila.

"But that's just insane!" said the Keeper in response.
"INSANELY BRILLIANT!" interrupted Hakramen and Reikiila tutted at her response.

"It's an interesting idea, but will it work?" asked Totomal calmly.

"Well, it has been done before. I saw it in this book where Amelia and Dothvera Cherama were writing together. She would make the book smaller for her to write in and then she would make it grow for the dragon, and both have written in it. It's crazy and it has both of their handwriting, but when Amelia made it smaller in the end, the magic has lasted. It's more stable a creation. Plus, I think it doesn't have the fear factor of being suddenly seen if it wears off."

The Keepers all looked at Bobby a little bit nervously. If they did this, they would be putting their lives into his hands. People could die in Shamlu. It was possible. It very rarely happened because of the magic of the place and the possibilities being endless there. Especially with an imaginer like Bobby by your side, but it was still possible.

Bobby knew he would need to soothe the Keepers minds about this and maybe even show them how possible it was. After they had left and had arranged another meeting, Bobby asked Hakramen if she could help him with something.

Of course, the Keeper was only too willing to help her friend. She headed to the towers with Bobby and the two of them began to set the plan into action. Bobby recited the words in his head, "Believe, Focus, Let go," he thought over and over again. This was going to be interesting. He was going to try and miniaturise himself.

Hakramen stood patiently while Bobby tried to believe that he could become smaller and smaller and smaller. He tried to focus on an image of himself becoming so tiny that Hakramen could hardly see him. He was trying his hardest, but he couldn't quite seem to let go and do this straight away, because it scared him to imagine himself that small. A few fears were in his mind about him being stood on by accident or ending up a tiny person forgotten about and left in Shamlu forever because Hakramen couldn't find him. This wasn't working. So, Bobby opened his eyes. Hakramen just stared at him.

"Well?" she asked.
"Well, maybe this is a crazy idea. What if you end up stepping on me or worse?"

"What's worse than me stepping on you?" asked Hakramen thinking out loud, "I mean, it seems like the most horrific thing that could happen, it's really awfu..."
"You're not helping!" interrupted Bobby who was feeling worse now.

"Well, maybe if we try to think of something to stop that happening?" Hakramen said.

"Maybe you can create a loud noise somehow, so that I know where you are, or... wait, I've got it! I'll need a magnifying glass. That'll do it!" smiled

Hakramen. "I won't move until I've found you. How about that?"

Bobby did feel a little better about that idea, but he also had this horrible image of Hakramen's humungous foot heading towards him and him screaming but her not hearing him. Realising he might end up bringing a Boglet to himself, he desperately tried to shut off that thought in his mind.

"Okay, and how about I get a trumpet or something so that I can make a noise and you can listen out for me?"
"If that makes you feel better then yes."

It didn't make Bobby feel that much better, but he tried to think of the reason why he wanted to do this in the first place. He tried to think of how amazing it would be to see his mum again. He wondered if she would notice how much he had changed. He pictured her smiling at him to check if he was well and happy. He honestly wasn't sure how much time had passed in his world. Time had kind of melted into one long moment here in Shamlu, but it had felt like so much had happened already. So many things had been and gone that it felt like he had been in Shamlu for an exceptionally long time.

"Well?" said Hakramen interrupting Bobby's thoughts.

Bobby closed his eyes. First, he imagined the trumpet and it gradually appeared and landed in front of him. He picked it up, took a deep breath in and tried not to be afraid and to believe. He could do this. Here, anything was possible. He focused. He tried not to think of anything else. He let go. He thought hard to imagine himself getting smaller. He pictured it happening. Then he knew something had happened because he heard the echoing sound of Hakramen above him.

Bobby didn't want to open his eyes. This was frightening. Hakramen was now a giant in front of him. He remembered the trumpet in his hand. He sounded it and Hakramen looked down her voice bellowing.

"I HEEEARR YOU BOBBBBY!" she said, not realising how loud her voice sounded. Bobby covered his ears.

Hakramen began to move closer to the sound. Bobby opened his eyes and was amazed by what he saw. The room was huge. Bobby was right in the middle of the huge stone floor of the towering room, and Hakramen was right there in front of him holding the magnifying glass and staring around the room clumsily. Bobby blew the trumpet once more.

Suddenly Hakramen stopped still and she leant down close to where Bobby was standing. He watched as she brought the magnifying glass closer and her huge eye, now magnified, also stared at him.

"Gotchya!" Hakramen smiled. She put her flat hand out and Bobby ran over to it and walked upon it. Hakramen began to laugh and her hand wobbled and Bobby fell over.

"It's tickling," she laughed. Bobby hung on for dear life, as Hakramen brought him closer to her.

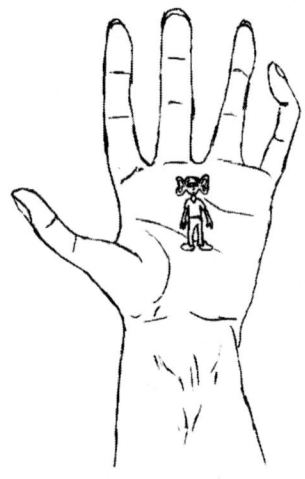

"What do I look like?" Bobby asked.

"Like..." Hakramen stopped momentarily to work out how best to describe the situation,

"...like a very tiny person," she looked closer, "with HUGE ears!" she exclaimed.

"What?" answered Bobby touching his ears. As he did, he noticed that they stretched out a lot further than before. His imagination had worked, but Bobby knew that he couldn't let Reikiila and Totomal see this. Bobby had to figure out a way to solve the ear problem before they walked in. But he was too late. They were already heading down the hall and Bobby could hear them.

Bobby decided that until he could sort out the big ear situation, he would need to hide it. Something he could easily think of was a hat. So, Bobby imagined one and placed it upon his head. Looking rather funny with a hat trying to cover his now humungous ears, Bobby panicked as the two Keepers headed in his direction.

Reikiila and Totomal were surprised to see Bobby in a hat. He had never worn one before, but they were too distracted by the size of Bobby to concern themselves about it now.

"Wow, I can't quite believe it..." said Reikiila, leaning down to look at Bobby, "Do you feel okay?"
"Of course, I feel great!" said Bobby, hoping his ears wouldn't pop out from underneath the hat.
"Do you think that we could do this?" asked Totomal.

"I think so!" called out Bobby.

The Keepers could just about hear the boy because of his size. He was extremely quiet to them, even though he was shouting.

Hakramen moved Bobby over to the bed and he began to shout about how wonderful this would be, and how it would work so beautifully and how this would be an amazing adventure, and that he could do this for everyone and that nothing could go wrong.

The Keepers listened to him intently as he yelled out his intentions for the next few days. He would increase himself in size and then he would begin work on the small plane that would be disguised as a small fly. Then once his flying contraption was complete, he would work on making it invisible anyway. Then he would fly out with the dragons and Totomal would fly the plane to follow the dragons, mapping the route to the mountains. From there, the Keepers would fly out immediately after Bobby's training to make sure that the goal was accomplished.

This was going to be EPIC!

As soon as Totomal and Reikiila left, Bobby and Hakramen sighed a huge sigh of relief at precisely the same time.

"Phew!" said Hakramen, "That was a close one!"

They were both thankful that Bobby's ears had not been noticed. Bobby hoped that the mistake wouldn't occur on the following miniaturisation, but he thought it was a small price to pay for getting himself home. He was quite sure the ears would go back to normal size once he returned to normal size.

He decided to try this out immediately and asked Hakramen to place him on the floor with enough room for him to grow back to his original size.

Hakramen placed the boy on the floor and stepped away from him. Bobby believed and this time because he knew it was possible, the creation happened almost immediately. The boy shot up and looked over to Hakramen who was looking a little shocked.

"What?" asked Bobby.
"Your ears!" she exclaimed.
"Oh no!" he said and as he felt along the sides of his ears, he realised they were not only large, they were now hanging down by his shoulders they were so big.

Bobby panicked.

This was going to take all night.

CHAPTER 18

Imagining, imagining, imagining

Bobby stayed up late trying to believe that his ears would go down. His desperation didn't help him to reduce the size of his ears quickly. After a long time of sitting there, imagining and dreaming himself with his original sized ears, the problem eventually disappeared. Even though he wasn't sure they were exactly the same size as before, at least they were no longer hanging near his shoulders.

Hakramen had fallen asleep on Bobby's bed and smiled with relief when she was awoken by Bobby.

"That's more like it!" she said, yawning. "Glad you deflated your ears Pocromethrah, you're a genius, this is going to be exciting!"

It was going to be exciting. This was going to be an adventure like no other that Bobby or any of the other Keepers would ever have been on. It was a privilege to know someone like Bobby, he was the kind of person that could do anything in Shamlu and Totomal and Reikiila were beginning to respect that fact. The boy was young, and he had a long way to go, but he was also extraordinarily talented at imagining things here. That was one of the most amazing things about being around him. The Keepers were beginning to see that with Pocromethrah by their side, anything really was possible.

Not only that, but Bobby was beginning to realise it too.

Dothvera Ferrucio was going to wake Bobby soon for his next day of training. He was tired and yawning a lot, so he imagined up a rather delicious breakfast and something he had not been allowed to try before at home with his mum – a cup of coffee with lots of sugar.

He had noticed that it was something his mother had often used to wake herself up in the mornings and she often joked that without her coffee she wouldn't be able to function, so Bobby was keen to try this coffee idea.

He drank the large mug of imagined coffee down and waited for it to take effect. As he flew with Dothvera Ferrucio to the training grounds he began to ask lots of questions and the dragon wasn't quite sure what was going on. Today Bobby seemed hyper.

"So, what are we doing today Dothvera?"
"Well, we'll let you know when we get there," the dragon replied.

"Is it going to be the dragon jumping again? Or are we going to practice the translating? Wait! No! I've learned translating, how about, is it something like imagining myself with wings? How cool would that be? That would be cool wouldn't it Dothvera?" the dragon tried to answer but before he could, Bobby started to talk again.

"You see, I've always wondered what it would be like to have wings, have you ever wondered what... Oh no, you have wings," the boy began to giggle at how funny what he had just said was, and then he burst out laughing and that continued until Dothvera Ferrucio reached the mountains.

The poor dragon was completely confused by Bobby's strange actions, after all the boy was usually polite and quiet but today, he was a little stir crazy.

Bobby who had never felt this alive before, couldn't quite believe what coffee was capable of. However, the effects didn't last for long.

While Dothvera Cherama was explaining about imagining things quickly and efficiently, Bobby began to feel ultra-tired. The caffeine was losing its kick and the boy began to yawn uncontrollably, not hearing a word that Dothvera Cherama was saying.

"Okay, let's begin!" the dragon said, knowing that Bobby hadn't heard a thing.

"Hmm!?" asked Bobby a little worried.

The dragons departed the field and took their place on the mountains above Bobby. The boy gulped. He wasn't quite sure what was about to happen.

Suddenly Dothvera Ferrucio began to pelt huge fireballs at Bobby and one landed so close to the boy that he jumped and ran from it. Thankfully, the dragon was a very good aim and knew exactly what he was trying to teach the boy. Also, without Bobby's knowledge, Dothvera Velara was on guard to protect the boy within inches of a fireball hitting him. So the dragons knew that he wasn't in danger. However, Bobby didn't know this and knew he had to act quickly. The fireballs began to come at him from all directions and Bobby tried to think quickly.

The best thing he could imagine for now was a wall of water around him, but he had no time to think about it, because a few fireballs were heading very much in his direction. Bobby closed his eyes, he panicked. He jumped out of the way of the other fireballs.

Then he imagined something simpler. He began to throw balls of water at the fireballs putting them out as they flew towards him. He tried to get himself in a bubble of water, but he could only manage to cover his head, not his whole body. He used the water over his head as a shield and began to destroy the fireballs until they stopped coming at him.

Then he took a deep breath and suddenly, he saw Dothvera Velara and Dothvera Ferrucio swap places and the water dragon began to pelt huge arrows of ice at the boy. Bobby couldn't believe his eyes. It felt like the dragons were trying to kill him, but Dothvera Ferrucio knew that if Bobby couldn't get the ice to melt or destroyed in time, he would easily be able to protect him. This was all calculated, but Bobby didn't know that.

Bobby ran and jumped and dodged as much as he could.

"Think Bobby, think!!" called out Dothvera Cherama.

The boy tried to think what would keep him safe and he imagined a sword and shield as quickly as possible. While they were being created he dodged, but as the shield formed itself, it was hit by a huge icy arrow and it broke apart.

Bobby kept running, he picked up the sword, and started to slice the arrows as they were coming closer to him. The dragons were impressed. Then when Bobby had hit most of the arrows down, Dothvera Potentioh stood in place and started to send down air that could sweep Bobby away and hit him at such a speed, he would not survive.

Bobby panicked. What could he do to stop fast and powerful gusts of air? He tried to think and ran to dodge things, but he fell to the ground after a short while and began to weep.

"I can't!" he cried.

Dothvera Potentioh sucked back the air and everything went silent again.

"You already have," said Dothvera Cherama. "You just fought off balls of the hottest, most deadliest fire and arrows that would have destroyed you in just one hit. It was just an idea that you needed Pocromethrah. I have found this very impressive. You are getting better, but you need to learn to trust in yourself."

"But what could I have done?" Bobby asked the wise dragon.
"Asked for help." the dragon answered, and he lifted his wing to show the three Keepers who had been watching the whole time without Bobby knowing.

"Hakramen, Reikiila, Totomal, you have a few seconds. Think!"

The noise began to lift and Dothvera Potentioh began to get himself ready to start again, meanwhile Dothvera Cherama readied himself to hit the air with a wall of stone to protect the Keepers if anything went wrong.

Hakramen ran over to Pocromethrah and picked him up. Totomal and Reikiila readied themselves for battle.

"Let's stay close!" shouted Reikiila.
"Pocromethrah! Build cover!" called Totomal.
"What kind of cover?"
"Anything!" the three Keepers shouted.

Bobby thought of a time when he was in a storm and his mother took him to the nearest church and they ran inside to take cover. He began to imagine a building and the Keepers kept close and tried to keep dodging the powerful gusts that were heading closer. Bobby found his answer and the building was being built but it was not quick enough. Dothvera Cherama put up the wall and it appeared inches away from the gust that was about to blow the Keepers to their deaths.

Bobby looked up.

"I'm not fast enough!" he called to Dothvera Cherama.

"You will be!" answered the dragon and took his place to challenge Pocromethrah next.

"This is insane!" called out Reikiila, "What are they doing?"

"Training Pocromethrah!!" answered Totomal. The Keepers all looked at Bobby in amazement. They had been trained to be Keepers and how to get into Shamlu, but they had not been trained like this.

Dothvera Cherama was readying himself and began to hit large lumps of earth at the four Keepers. Bobby's face was filled with fear. Hakramen turned to Bobby and shouted over to him.

"YOU CAN DO THIS POCROMETHRAH!!" she called as big, huge lumps of earth shattered on the ground all around them.

"Do what?"
"Build us cover Pocromethrah, but quickly!!"

Bobby listened to his mind. He thought of an idea of building a huge metal frame around everyone, like those buildings his grandfather had told him about that everyone had used in the war when bombs were being sent down towards them.

Bobby readied his mind, he begged that it be built quickly, and he closed his eyes.

"OVER THERE!!" shouted Reikiila and when Bobby opened his eyes, he saw an actual fallout shelter just across from them all. Dothvera Cherama continued to pelt the earth towards the Keepers as they ran fast towards the fallout shelter.

Hakramen tripped and fell as she was running and Pocromethrah picked her up and ran slowly with her, imagining a shield that went around them both protecting them. As they ran, they noticed that the sounds went quiet. Bobby and Hakramen were inside a bubble-like shield that had stopped them moving any further. Totomal and Reikiila were in the fallout shelter, with absolute shock and amazement in their eyes, watching on from the doorway.

Pocromethrah had saved them all and himself today.

"You are getting stronger." said Dothvera Cherama. "This first part of your training is complete. We will return when you are ready for part two. Until then Pocromethrah, it is books and yourself that will have to train you."

Bobby looked at the other Keepers. If they couldn't go out training again, they would never find a way for Bobby to get home. The Keepers headed back to the towers and they all headed to the dragon's library together.

"Well, I guess that's it!" said Reikiila.
"What's it?" asked Hakramen.
"Well, we can't find our way back there now,"

Bobby sat at the desk looking defeated. Totomal sat next to him and then handed him something. It was a compass.

"North West." said Totomal. Bobby smiled from ear to ear.

"You're a genius! We can map our way there now we know that it's north-west, we CAN do this! How did you know?"

"I didn't, I just thought it was a good time to see if my compass would work in Shamlu and it does," answered Totomal.

The Keeper smiled at how happy Pocromethrah was with him, but he had something more to say.

"We must leave soon. What you did today proved your skills are growing and we will need you back. The sooner you leave, the sooner you will return."

The boy nodded. Sometimes Bobby didn't want to come back. He felt the responsibility of saving everyone heavy on his heart. Sometimes all he wanted to do was to play and have fun and forget about Shamlu. He also realised that his grandfather and his great grandmother would be watching over him right now and they would want him to keep Shamlu safe and to look after the Keepers. This was his destiny, and he couldn't ignore it anymore.

Bobby knew that his creative skills were getting stronger. He was beginning to believe that his imagination was immensely powerful, and that he was using it to his advantage more and more. He could create this small flying contraption quickly and he could disguise it as a small fly, and he could make it invisible.

He decided to head back to his room and begin.

CHAPTER 19

The invisible flying contraption

Bobby spent a lot of time thinking about this. It would need to be small enough to pass by the dragons unnoticed and invisible. He wouldn't worry too much about the invisibility, but he would have to test it. If the magic wore out, then at least the flying creature would be disguise enough.

The Keepers wanted to make the journey tomorrow, first thing. They had asked Bobby to make the flying contraption by then. Bobby felt a lot of pressure. He had to get this right.

He began working on the fly plane and imagined all the gears working perfectly and things all being the right size. He made a drawing of how the plane would look on the inside and how it would appear from the outside. He called it the

'FLY PLANE' and tried to draw it in detail as best he could.

Bobby had found out a little about planes from Totomal and Reikiila. He had also been taught a little by his grandfather who knew how to fly planes and would often teach him little things about them.

Bobby imagined all the buttons, the lever to guide the plane and the fuel tank being able to fill itself up automatically by magic, and the outside being hairy with big bug eyes and the wings being hidden by what looked like a flies wings. The black hairy disguise would not get in the way of the plane being flown. The eyes would act as a big dark window, a bit like tinted windows on cars. The landing wheels would be hidden by the hairy legs of a fly.

This was truly a well imagined flying contraption.

When Bobby looked at the pea sized flying contraption through his magnifying glass, he couldn't really tell if it was built to his expectations. The eyes looked real and the hairy body of the fly was definitely a good disguise, but Bobby didn't know for sure if anything inside the plane would work. He decided to make the plane invisible and see what would happen.

As soon as he finished imagining, Bobby opened his eyes. The pea sized, fly like, plane was no longer in the palm of his hand. Or at least he couldn't see it. The weird thing was, he could feel it. He put his finger in the palm of his hand and rolled the fly plane around, but then he felt it roll off his hand and onto the floor.

Bobby couldn't believe it. Had he just lost the only really awesome flying contraption he had ever created, because he had made it invisible?

He tried to feel around on the floor but couldn't feel anything. Then he heard someone.

"Hey how's the creating going?"
"NOOOOOOOO!!" Bobby shouted at Hakramen. The girl stopped still in a bit of a shock.

"Everything okay Bobby?"

"Stay still, I've lost the plane!"

"Oh, my Goodness, No!"

"Just, stay still. It's ridiculously tiny," said Bobby nervously.

"Why don't you try to uninvisible it?" asked Hakramen, who, although her English hadn't quite made sense, had said something that made perfect sense.

"Okay but you can't come in until I find it," said Bobby to Hakramen who then sat in the doorway of his tower bedroom.

Bobby closed his eyes and pictured the plane being back to where it was in his hands, visible to him and perfect. The magic worked. Bobby was getting much quicker at this.

"Wow" said Hakramen staring at the tiny plane that looked just like a small fly in Bobby's hand. "That's amazing! We should try it!"

"Not without us!" said Reikiila with Totomal right behind him.

"I guess this is going to happen early eh?" said Hakramen.

The three Keepers stared at the small flying contraption and stood together. Bobby was concerned that he hadn't tested things, but he also knew that he wanted to get home as soon as he could. He put his fearful thoughts aside and followed the keepers.

"Maybe we should hold hands just in case," Totomal said. Reikiila didn't like the idea of it but even he ended up holding hands with Totomal and Hakramen. Bobby held Hakramen's hand and Totomal's and they all closed their eyes. Bobby prayed that this plan was going to work and started his imagining. "Focus, believe, let go." he repeated in his mind and the magic started to respond.

Shrinking felt odd. The Keepers all let go of each other's hands and lost their balance a little bit, but then when they gathered their senses, they all began to stare at each other. Bobby finally opened his eyes.

"Oh dear!" he said.
"Oh dear!?" said Reikiila, "Oh dear!? Is that all you can say?"
Bobby looked around; everyone's ears were incredibly large for the size of their bodies. This was awkward.

"Change it! Change it now!" said Reikiila.
"I'll try," answered Bobby who was trying to imagine everyone's ears getting smaller, but then they all began to get smaller and smaller and

smaller and only finished when they were even smaller than they should have been.

Now everyone had really bad hearing and very small ears.

"CHANGE IT!!" called out Reikiila.

"IT'S NOT WORKING!" shouted Bobby.

"Let's just all calm down," said Totomal.

"WHAT?!!?" everyone shouted in return.

Bobby knew this wasn't going to work. They needed to hear each other. He tried to imagine everyone's ears being the perfect size for their body and gradually they did begin to grow, but they were still a little too large. Just not as large as they had been at the beginning.

"Let's look inside!" said Hakramen moving on from the previous situation quite quickly. She was easily distracted, but that helped Bobby.

"You need teaching, young man," said Reikiila.

"Slow down Reikiila," Totomal said, trying to keep the peace.

"It's never happened before!" said Bobby.

"Never happened before? Then why were you in a hat last time we saw you this size hmm?"

Bobby decided that the best thing was to just shut up. He probably wasn't going to win this one and the main thing was that everyone was small enough and now they could get into the flying contraption.

Bobby then realised his mistake.

The fly plane was still in his hand. He had kept it in his hand the whole time and it was even more miniscule than before. He couldn't believe this but he would have to admit it, so that he could make the plane large enough again. This was going to be embarrassing.

"Okay, um. I just need to make the flying contraption bigger because I just miniaturised it along with us,"
"WHAT?" called out Reikiila in a rage.
"I'll sort it out." said Bobby staring directly into the Keepers eyes.

Bobby took himself over to an area on the stone floor where there was plenty of space and imagined. Sure enough, the FLY PLANE grew, and it grew perfectly.

Everybody looked up at it. Bobby sighed in relief.

"Amazing, well done!" said Totomal.
"Wooooow!" said Hakramen.
Reikiila said nothing.

Bobby was rather proud of this fantastic creation of his. He had never even seen a plane back at home, and here he was standing in front of one he'd just created.

"Is it invisible?" asked Reikiila.

"No, but I don't think it will need to be. Plus I don't have the time to test it." Reikiila smiled, as though he was happy to know that. Bobby figured it must have been because he had noticed that it looked like he'd failed at something. The Keeper liked to see that happen to him.

Totomal called Bobby and Reikiila into the plane. It was time for take-off.

"It's all perfect, the sizes are spot on. Well imagined Pocromethrah." said Totomal who was a keen pilot.

The seats in the plane were just as Bobby had imagined them, all four in a row and right at the front. Everyone had a seatbelt for safety and the plane had a built-in compass.

"Wait!" said Bobby realising there was something he'd forgotten, "...the map!"

The Keepers all looked at each other for ideas. Then Totomal said something that sounded like an idea that Hakramen could have come up with.

"Pocromethrah, can you bring it here? Replicate it? Make it the right size and bring it here?" Bobby panicked. He wasn't sure he could. Moving objects around wasn't something he had tried.

"I'm not sure," said Bobby to Totomal, with worry in his eyes.
"Just try it and if not, we'll go and get it,"

Bobby spent some time trying to imagine the map making its way to them, but he couldn't quite get it to appear. Totomal started the plane up and decided that they would go and get the map. It would be easier, but he thanked Bobby for trying.

As the Keepers lifted the plane up, they noticed a map hit the outside window and then fly away. It was massive.

"That was it!!" cried out Hakramen. "Open the door!" she called.
"You're crazy!" cried out Reikiila.

Hakramen trusted herself and opened the door of the plane, sending huge amounts of air rushing in through the door. On the air, flew a map that landed right at Reikiila's feet before Hakramen pulled the door to a close.

Bobby picked up the map that had conveniently shrunk to the right size just in time.

261

"This IS it!" he smiled.

As the Keepers flew smoothly out of the tower windows and into the Shamlu skies, Bobby couldn't believe how much he had played a part in the whole creation of this. Here he was, a ten year old boy, with three other Keepers.

Even Reikiila sitting by his side flying into the skies, so small that they could fit into this fly-sized contraption and so well disguised that no one would be able to work out that they were in here. This WAS incredible and Bobby or should he have called himself Pocromethrah, had done it.

The map didn't have North, South, East or West on it like maps usually did, so Bobby knew that they would have to follow the map closely after they arrived at the mountains. Totomal continued to fly North-west.

All of a sudden, Hakramen cried out, "We've made it!" and everyone looked down. From this size, the mountains looked ridiculously huge. Even flying over them, it seemed like a very long time. Totomal asked Bobby for the map and he began to study it carefully.

"So, if we head towards that line of trees, and then towards the safe resting place, from there it seems pretty straight forward," Totomal told Bobby and Bobby smiled in return.

This was his journey home. He was scared about what lay ahead when he returned to Shamlu, but now he was on his way to see his mum and to find her and to hug her. He hoped he'd find her just where she was, downstairs.

As Bobby finally reached Elsanthah, his eyes lit up with joy. He had been waiting for this moment. This was everything he'd been wanting. The edge of Shamlu looked strange. It was like the space was so magical it was almost shimmering. The green grass seemed very much like the grass in Shamlu, but it was bright and shining as though it was directly in the sunlight.

As the plane rested itself on the ground, Bobby couldn't wait to run outside and reach the doorway to his homeland.

"Wait!" called out Hakramen running after him and hugging him tightly, "say goodbye," she said. Bobby nodded.

"I wasn't going to just leave you, you know," he answered. Hakramen began to cry tears of sadness, as Bobby said his goodbyes. He hugged Totomal next but when he looked for Reikiila, the old man was nowhere to be seen.

Bobby panicked. He hoped the Keeper was safe. Then he turned round hearing the old man's voice in the distance.

"NOT SO FAST BOBBY!" called out Reikiila, grinning at what he had just done. The four dragons were right behind him. Dothvera Cherama stood in front of the boy who was just about to step through into his own world.

Bobby knelt down in defeat.

He couldn't believe that after all he had been through, he wouldn't be able to see his mother. Reikiila laughed and Hakramen threw herself at the old man angrily, but Totomal held her back.

"He's not worth it." Totomal whispered into Hakramen's ear.

Reikiila continued to laugh until Dothvera Cherama spoke.

"I am glad that you find the betrayal of your friend amusing Reikiila." the man went quiet.

"Hakramen, you know how to treat people. Pick our friend up from his knees." Hakramen picked Bobby up off the floor and looked at him in concern.

"Bobby, I have one thing to ask of you, before you go."

"Go?" asked Reikiila, "But you have him, he's not going anywhere!"

"Isn't he?" asked the wise dragon. Bobby paid attention. Not quite believing what he was hearing. Were the dragons going to let him go home?

Reikiila watched on in fear and despair as his future saviour was handed a key to Shamlu to ensure his safe return.

"Yes," answered Bobby. ???

"Make sure you return." upon saying this the dragon stepped aside and Bobby said the words "Remero, Remero, Remero," and closed his eyes imagining and stepped forward.

"Goodbye Pocromethrah." he heard and then everything went quiet again.

Bobby opened his eyes. His room was just as messy as he had left it. He looked at the time. He ran downstairs and found his mum who was still polishing the front room table. He ran up to her and hugged her so tightly she became immediately overwhelmed with emotion.

"Mum!" he said.

"Bobby??" Jenny asked, looking in her son's eyes and wiping away the tears.

"I love you mum."

THE END

What will Bobby do next?

POCROMETHRAH the next book is on its way!